Bodily Secrets

WILLIAM TREVOR

Bodily Secrets

GREAT LOVES

PENGUIN BOOKS

Published by the Penguin Group
Penguin Books Ltd, 80 Strand, London WC2R 0RL, England
Penguin Group (USA) Inc., 375 Hudson Street, New York, New York 10014, USA
Penguin Group (Canada), 90 Eglinton Avenue East, Suite 700, Toronto, Ontario, Canada M4P 2Y3
(a division of Pearson Penguin Canada Inc.)
Penguin Ireland, 25 St Stephen's Green, Dublin 2, Ireland
(a division of Penguin Books Ltd)
Penguin Group (Australia), 250 Camberwell Road, Camberwell, Victoria 3124, Australia
(a division of Pearson Australia Group Pty Ltd)
Penguin Books India Pvt Ltd, 11 Community Centre, Panchsheel Park, New Delhi – 110 017, India
Penguin Group (NZ), 67 Apollo Drive, Rosedale, North Shore 0632, New Zealand
(a division of Pearson New Zealand Ltd)
Penguin Books (South Africa) (Pty) Ltd, 24 Sturdee Avenue,
Rosebank, Johannesburg 2196, South Africa

Penguin Books Ltd, Registered Offices: 80 Strand, London WC2R 0RL, England

www.penguin.com

All stories taken from *The Collected Stories of William Trevor* first published in Great Britain
by Penguin Books 1992
First published in the United States of America by
Viking Penguin, a division of Penguin Books USA Inc. 1992
This selection published in Penguin Books 2007

1

Copyright © William Trevor, 1992
All rights reserved

Typeset by Rowland Phototypesetting Ltd, Bury St Edmunds, Suffolk
Printed in England by Clays Ltd, St Ives plc

978-0-141-03323-5

Contents

William Trevor was born in Mitchelstown, County Cork, in 1928 and spent his childhood in provincial Ireland. He studied at Trinity College, Dublin. He has written many novels, and won many prizes including the Whitbread Book of the Year Award. *The Hill Bachelors* (2000), a collection of short stories, won both the PEN/Macmillan Silver Pen Award for Short Stories and the *Irish Times* Irish Literature Prize for Fiction in 2001. *The Story of Lucy Gault* (2002), was shortlisted for the Man Booker Prize for Fiction. William Trevor's latest books are *A Bit On the Side* (2004), on the theme of adultery; *The Dressmaker's Child* (2005); and *Cheating at Canasta* (2007).

Many of William Trevor's stories have appeared in *The New Yorker* and other magazines. He has also written plays for the stage, and for radio and television. In 2002 William Trevor was awarded an honorary knighthood in recognition of his services to literature.

The Day We Got Drunk on Cake

Garbed in a crushed tweed suit, fingering the ragged end of a tie that might have already done a year's service about his waist, Swann de Lisle uttered a convivial obscenity in the four hundred cubic feet of air they euphemistically called my office. I had not seen him for some years: he is the kind of person who is often, for no reason one can deduce, out of the country. In passing, one may assume that his lengthy absences are due in some way to the element of disaster that features so commandingly in his make-up.

I should have known when I saw him standing there that I must instantly be on my guard. In my prevailing condition of emotional delicacy I could not hope to cope with whatever entertainment Swann had in mind for me. For, to give him his due, Swann never came empty-handed. Swann was a great one for getting the best out of life; and he offered one, invariably, a generous part of his well-laid plans. This time, he explained, he was offering me an attractive afternoon. In turn, I explained that I did not feel like an attractive afternoon, that I was too busy to gild the hours in the manner he was suggesting. But Swann was sitting down, well entrenched; and in the end he talked me into it.

I wrote a note and put it on my typewriter: *Tuesday*

I

p.m. Am under surgeon's knife. Then I made a telephone call.

'Lucy?'

'Hullo, Mike.'

'How are you?'

'Very well, Mike. How are you?'

'Very well, too. Just thought I'd ring –'

'Thank you, Mike.'

'We must meet again soon.'

'Yes, we must.'

'I'd invite you to lunch only an old and valued friend has just transpired.'

'That's nice for you.'

'Well, yes.'

'Thanks for ringing, Mike.'

'Goodbye, Lucy.'

'Goodbye, Mike.'

Swann was drawing designs on the varnish of my desk with a straightened-out paper-clip.

'That wasn't your wife,' he said.

'Wife? Far from it.'

'You haven't married or anything?'

'No.'

'Good. I've got a couple in a hostelry. They tell me they know you.' We sauntered out into the September sun to meet them.

I have always wanted to invent pert shorthand typists with good figures and pretty lips whose heads may easily be turned by the crisp jingle of money, jolly girls who have done the stint at Pitman's and do not believe in anticipating marriage. It might quite easily have been such companions with whom we found ourselves wasting away that afternoon. As it happened, it was Margo and Jo, a smart pair who drew pictures for the glossy magazines.

'When I was eleven,' Jo told me, 'I wrote this children's book and drew all the pictures. Somebody published it, and that of course made me unpopular with everyone.'

'You must have been hugely clever.'

'No, honestly. It was terribly bad, as you can imagine. Just chance that it got published.'

'Words,' said Margo, 'mean a lot to Jo. She has a real sense.'

'She's bonkers,' said Swann.

'For God's sake, Swann,' said Margo.

Jo and Swann moved together. Swann was bored and he began to tell Jo a joke. Margo said, specifically to me: 'Jo is the most talented person I've ever met.' I nodded, not caring one way or the other. The bar was full of uniformed men: dark grey suits, waistcoats, white shirts, striped ties of some club or school.

'Have a drink, Margo?'

Margo said that was a good idea and I squeezed through to the wet counter and floated a ten-shilling note on a pool of beer. When I returned to her Margo said:

'Tell me straight, what do you think of Nigel?'

Nigel? Playing for time I sipped my beer, wondering why I drank the stuff since I disliked it so much. I said:

'Oh, I like Nigel.'

'Do you *really*?'

'Well, he's all right. I mean –'

'Sometimes, Mike, I think Nigel is the most awful bore.'

I remembered. Nigel was plump and talkative. Nigel would tell you anything you might ever wish to know. When Nigel got going there was, in truth, no stopping Nigel. Nigel was Margo's husband.

I drank some more beer. It was cold and tasteless. I said nothing.

'Nigel and I had a barney last night.'

'Oh God!'

Margo told me about the barney. I listened deject-edly. Then I bought some more drink, and this time I changed mine to whiskey. Someone had once told me that Jo had a husband too. Both marriages were considered to be heading for the rocks.

Suddenly Margo stopped about Nigel. She leered at me and said something I didn't catch. From the next few sentences, I realized she was telling me I'd make a good husband.

'I suppose I would,' I said.

'I'm not in love with you or anything,' Margo said, swaying.

'Of course not.'

After the pub we went off to have some lunch. All the way in the taxi I thought about Lucy.

We went to an Italian place in Soho that was too expensive and not particularly good. Swann told us the history of his life and ate only series of cassatas. I found a telephone on the stairs and rang up Lucy.

'Hullo, Lucy. What are you doing?'

'What d'you mean, what am I doing? I'm standing here talking to you on the telephone.'

'I'm getting drunk with people in Soho.'

'Well, that's nice for you.'

'Is it? Wish you were here.'

Lucy would be bored by this. 'I've been reading *Adam Bede*,' she said.

'A good story.'

'Yes.'

'Have you had lunch?'

'I couldn't find anything. I had some chocolate.'

'I telephoned to see how you were.'

'I'm fine, thanks.'

'I wanted to hear your voice.'

'Oh come off it. It's just a voice.'

'Shall I tell you about it?'

'I'd rather you didn't. I don't know why.'

'Shall we meet some time?'

'I'm sure we shall.'

'I'll ring you when I'm sober.'

'Do that. I must get back to *Adam Bede*.'

'Goodbye.'

'Goodbye.'

I replaced the receiver and stood there looking down the steep stairs. Then I descended them.

'What on earth shall we do now?' Swann said. 'It's four o'clock.'

'I want to talk to Mike,' Margo announced. 'Nobody's to listen.'

I sat beside her and she began to speak in a limping whisper. 'I want your advice about Nigel, Mike.'

'Honestly, I scarcely know him.'

'Doesn't matter. Look, I think there's something the matter with Nigel.'

I asked her to be specific. Instead she turned her assertion into a question. 'Mike, do *you* think there's something wrong with Nigel?'

'Well –'

'Be frank now.'

'I tell you, I don't know him. For all I know he may have an artificial stomach.'

'Nigel hasn't an artificial stomach, actually.'

'Good.'

'I don't know why you should think that about him. He doesn't even have trouble with his stomach.'

'Well, then, what's the matter with the man?'

'I think he's probably mental.'

'Well, for God's sake get him attended to, Margo.'

'You think I should?'

'Certainly I do. Unless you like his being mental.'

Margo giggled. She said:

'He's taken to doing such odd things. I mean, I don't know where this is going to stop.'

'Odd things like what?'

'Like bringing home elderly women. He comes in with these women, explaining that he has been attending some meeting with them and has brought them back for coffee. It's quite alarming – Nigel with four or five old ladies trailing behind him. They stay for ages. I've no idea where he gets them from. I think he imagines he's being kind.'

'What does Nigel say?'

'He says they haven't finished their meeting. They just sit around writing little notes. Nobody *says* anything.'

'I think it's all very interesting. I'm sure there's some quite simple explanation. I don't think you've really investigated the matter, Margo.'

'Let's leave this place,' Swann said.

We went to another place, called the Blue Goat. It was one of those clubs where you can drink in the afternoon without having to watch striptease. Margo tried to go on about Nigel, but I said firmly that I didn't want to hear anything more about Nigel. I talked to Jo.

'Jo,' I said, 'do you know a girl called Lucy Anstruth?'

'Small, plump, balding a little?'

'No. Lucy is a very beautiful person.'

'Not the same girl.'

'Tall, fair, very blue eyes. Moves like a cat.'

'Don't know her.'

'She says unexpected things. She's half Swedish or something.'

'Mike, would you guess I was half Welsh?'

'No. I want to ask you about Lucy –'

'But I don't know her.'

'I don't know what to do about Lucy.'

'You sound like Margo. Margo doesn't know what to do about Nigel. Nobody knows what to do about anyone else. God! May I have some more vodka?'

'Yes. As I say –'

'I want a triple vodka.'

I ordered the vodka. Beside us, Swann and Margo

were sitting in preoccupied silence; they weren't even listening to what we were saying. Margo caught my eye and opened her mouth to speak. I turned my back and handed Jo her drink.

'Something's the matter with Margo's husband,' Jo said. 'Poor Margo's terribly worried.'

'Yes, I know all about it. Margo has been telling me.'

'I like Nigel, you know.'

'Perhaps you can help him straighten himself out. We were talking about something else. I was telling you –'

'Seems Nigel brings women home.'

'Yes I know, Jo.'

'Bit rough on Margo.'

Margo heard this. She shouted: 'What's rough on Margo?' and then the conversation became general. I went away to telephone Lucy.

'Lucy?'

'Hullo. Is that Mike?'

'Yes.'

'Hullo, Mike.'

'Hullo, Lucy.'

'How are you?'

'I'm feeling funny. But Lucy?'

'Yes?'

'I'm not trying to *be* funny. I'm not being amusing.'

'Where are you?'

'In the Blue Goat.'

'Wherever's that?'

'It's lined with leopard skin. Jo and Margo and Swann are here too.'

'Who are they?'

'Just other people.'

'Nice of you to ring, Mike.'

'Margo's husband Nigel brings women home. I wondered perhaps if you had a word of advice I could give her. She's worried about the women. They come in groups.'

'Oh, Mike, I don't know about things like that. I wouldn't know what to do. Honestly.'

'Sorry, Lucy; I just thought you might.'

'The doorbell's ringing. Goodbye, Mike. If I were you I'd go home.'

Swann said he wanted tea. We left the Blue Goat and walked in dazzling sunshine towards Floris.

Margo began again about Nigel.

Swann said he knew a man who would do Nigel a world of good. He couldn't remember the treatment this man offered, but he said it was highly thought of.

I went away to telephone Lucy.

'Lucy?'

A man's voice answered. I said: 'May I speak to Lucy? Is that the right number?'

The man didn't reply and in a moment Lucy came on. 'Is that Mike again?'

'Hullo, Lucy. How are you?'

'I'm fine, Mike.'

'Good.'

'Mike, you telephoned me at four fifteen. Do you know what time it is now?'

'What time is it now?'

'Four thirty-five.'

'Am I being a nuisance, is that it?'

'No, no. Just, is there anything I can do for you? I mean, do you want something and feel unable to express yourself?'

'I'm bored. I'm with these people. Lucy.'

'Yes?'

'Who's that in your flat?'

'A friend called Frank. You don't know him.'

'What's he doing there?'

'What d'you mean, what's he doing?'

'Well –'

'Look, I'll ask him. Frank, what are you doing?'

'What's he say?'

'He says he's making a cup of tea.'

'I'm having tea too. In Floris. I wish you were here.'

'Goodbye, Mike.'

'Don't go, Lucy.'

'Goodbye, Mike.'

'Goodbye, Lucy.'

When I got back to the others I found them laughing in an uproarious manner. Swann said the cake they were eating was making them drunk. 'Smell it,' he said. It smelt of rum. I tasted some: it tasted of rum too. We all ate a lot of the cake, laughing at the thought of getting drunk on cake. We ordered some more, and told the waitress it was delicious. When the enthusiasm had melted a bit Swann said:

'Mike, we want your advice about Margo's husband.'

'I've told Margo –'

'No, Mike – seriously now. You know about these things.'

'Why do you think I know about these things? I do not know about these things.'

'All right, Mike, I'll tell you. Margo's husband Nigel keeps turning up with groups of old females. Margo's worried in case the thing develops a bit – you know, tramps, grocers, one-legged soldiers. What d'you think she should do?'

'I don't know what Margo should do. Margo, I don't know what you should do. Except perhaps ask Nigel what he's up to. In the meantime, have some more cake.'

'Now there's an idea,' Swann shouted excitedly. 'Margo love, why don't you ask old Nigel what he's up to?'

Jo hacked affectionately at my face with her great spiked fingers. I guessed it was an expression of admiration rather than attack because she smiled as she did so.

'But all Nigel says,' Margo said, 'is that they haven't finished their meeting.'

'Ah yes,' said Swann, 'but you don't press him. You don't say: "What meeting?" You don't indicate that you are in the dark as to the nub of their business. Nigel may well imagine that you accept the whole state of affairs without question and expect little else of married life. When you were at the Gents,' Swann said to me, 'Margo confessed she was worried.'

'She had previously confessed as much to me. I wasn't at the Gents. I was making a telephone call.'

'Shall *I* do that?' Margo said. 'Shall I ring up Nigel and ask him to explain everything?'

We all nodded. Margo rose, hesitated, and sat down again. She said she couldn't. She explained she was too shy to telephone her husband in this way. She turned to me.

'Mike, would you do it?'

'Me?'

'Mike, would you telephone?'

'Are you asking me to telephone your husband and inquire about his relationship with some elderly women who are entirely unknown to me?'

'Mike, for my sake.'

'Think of the explanations it would involve me in. Think of the confusion. Nigel imagining I was the husband of one of these women. Nigel imagining I was the police. Nigel asking me question after question. For goodness' sake, how do you think I would get some kind of answer out of *him*?'

Swann said: 'All you have to do is to say: "Is that Nigel? Now look here, Nigel, what's all this I hear about these women who come to your house at all hours of the day and night?" Say you represent the Ministry of Pensions.'

'I can't address the man as Nigel and then say I'm from the Ministry of Pensions.'

'Mike, Margo's husband's name *is* Nigel. He'll be expecting you to address him as Nigel. If you don't address him as Nigel, he'll simply tell you to go to hell. He'll say you've got a wrong number.'

'So I say: "Hullo, Nigel, this is the Ministry of Pensions." The man'll think I'm crazy.'

Margo said: 'Mike, you just do it your own way. Take no notice of Swann. Swann's been eating too much cake. Come on, you know where the telephone is.' She gave me a piece of paper with a number on it.

'Oh God,' I said; and unable to bear it any longer I borrowed fourpence and marched off to the telephone.

'Hullo?' said the voice at the other end.

'Hullo. Can I speak to Lucy? Please.'

'Hullo,' Lucy said.

'Hullo, Lucy.'

'Well?' said Lucy.

'It's Mike.'

'I know it's Mike.'

'They wanted me to telephone this man I was telling you about, but I can't go telephoning people in this way –'

'Why don't you go home to bed?'

'Because I wouldn't sleep. Remember the man with the elderly women? Well, they wanted me to telephone him and ask him what he's up to. Lucy, I can't do that, can I?'

'No, quite honestly I don't believe you can.'

'They told me to pose as the Ministry of Pensions.'

'Goodbye, Mike.'

'Just a – Lucy?'

'Yes?'

'Isn't that man still there?'

'Which man is this?'

'The man in your flat.'

'Frank. He's still here.'

'Who is he, Lucy?'

'He's called Frank.'

'Yes, but what does he do?'

'I don't know what he does. Frank, what do you do? For a living? He says he's a – what, Frank? A freight agent, Mike.'

'A freight agent.'

'Goodbye.'

'Goodbye, Lucy.'

When I arrived back at the tea-table everyone was very gay. Nobody asked me what Nigel had said. Swann paid the bill and said he was anxious to show us a display of Eastern horrors somewhere in Euston and would afterwards take us to a party. In the taxi Margo said:

'What did Nigel say?'

'He was out.'

'Was there no reply?'

'A woman answered. She said I was interrupting the meeting. I said "What meeting?" but she wanted to know who I was before she would answer that. I said I was the Ministry of Pensions and she said "Oh my God", and rang off.'

We were hours early for the party, but nobody seemed to mind. I helped a woman in slacks to pour bottles of wine into a crock. Swann, Margo and Jo played with a tape-recorder, and after a time the woman's husband arrived and we all went out to eat.

About eight, people began to arrive. The place filled with tobacco smoke, music and fumes; and the party began to swing along at a merry enough pace. A girl in ringlets talked to me earnestly about love. I think she must have been feeling much the same as I was, but I didn't fancy her as a soulmate, not even a temporary one. She said: 'It seems to me that everyone has a quality that can get the better of love. Is stronger, you see. Like pride. Or honesty. Or moral – even intellectual, even emotional – integrity. Take two people in love. The only thing that can really upset things is this personal quality in one of them. Other people don't come into it at all. Except in a roundabout way – as instruments of jealousy, for instance. Don't you agree?'

I wasn't sure about anything, but I said yes.

'Another thing about love,' the girl with the ringlets said, 'is its extraordinary infection. Has it ever occurred to you that when you're in love with someone you're really wanting to be loved yourself? Because that, of course, is the natural law. I mean, it would be odd if every time one person loved another person the first person wasn't loved in return. There's only a very tiny percentage of that kind of thing.'

An aggressive young man, overhearing these remarks, began to laugh. He went on laughing, looking at the girl in ringlets and looking at me.

I went away and filled my glass from the crock, and asked a pretty middle-aged woman what she did. Her answer was coy; I smiled and passed on. Margo caught my arm and dragged me off to a corner. 'Mike, you'll ring Nigel again?'

'I've been thinking about that,' I said. 'Honestly, I don't think I can interfere.'

'Oh but, dear, you promised.'

'Promised? I didn't promise anything.'

'Oh Mike.'

'Really, the whole affair – oh all right.'

'Now, Mike?'

'All right. Now.'

'Lucy?'

'Is that Mike?'

'Who else?'

'Who indeed? Where are you now?'

'I'm at a party.'

'A good party?'

'Yes, I suppose so. Why don't you come along?'

'I can't, Mike. I'm doing things.'

'With the bloody freight agent, I suppose.'

'The what agent?'

'Freight. Your friend the freight agent. Frank.'

'He's not a freight agent. He's in publishing.'

'What'd he say he was a freight agent for?'

A lengthy explanation followed. Calling himself a freight agent was a sample of Frank's humour. I thought about this as I made my way back to Margo.

'What'd he say, Mike?'

'A woman said Nigel wasn't in.'

'Is that all?'

'I said the house was being watched. I said the local authorities weren't at all happy.'

'What'd she say?'

'She began to moan, so I said "I mean it," and rang off.'

'Thank you, Mike.'

'That's all right. Any time.'

Swann joined us and Margo said: 'Mike's been on to Nigel again. Mike's being wonderful.'

Swann patted me on the back and said: 'Any joy?'

Margo started to tell him. I went away.

Jo was pretending to listen to a couple of men who were between them retailing a complicated story. She said to me in a low voice: 'Don't worry about Margo. I'll see she comes through the other side.'

I stared at her, wondering why she should imagine I was worried about Margo. 'I'm sure you will, Jo,' I said.

'Trust Jo,' she whispered.

I said I considered her a trustworthy person. I began to elaborate on the thought. One of the men said: 'D'you mind, old boy?'

I shrugged and pushed a path back to the telephone. I dialled three times to be certain, but on each occasion there was no reply.

A ragged form of dancing was now taking place. Pausing by the crock, I found myself once again in the company of the girl with the ringlets. She smiled at me and in a boring way I said: 'Do you know a girl called Lucy Anstruth?'

The girl with the ringlets shook her head. 'Should I?'

'I suppose not,' I said. The girl examined me closely and passed on.

I went upstairs and discovered a quiet room with a

bed in it. A lamp on a dressing-table gave out a weak light. The bed, which looked comfortable, was almost in darkness. I stretched out on it, welcoming the gloom. In a few moments I dropped off to sleep. When I awoke the luminous dial of my watch indicated that I had been asleep for two hours. Two girls were tidying their faces at the dressing-table. They drew head-scarves with horses on them from their handbags and placed them about their heads. They spoke in a whisper and left the room. I lay there considering the events of the day and wondering how I was going to feel about them at breakfast. How one feels at breakfast about the preceding day has always seemed to be important to me.

A man with a glass in his hand entered the room and placed himself before the mirror on the dressing-table. He combed his hair and tightened his tie. Then he took a handkerchief from his pocket and wrapped it around his right forefinger. He inserted this into each ear, twisting his forefinger back and forth. He remarked to himself on the outcome of this operation, examining his handkerchief. I closed my eyes; when I opened them he was gone. I lit a cigarette and set off to the telephone again.

'What is it?' a voice said. It was the publishing man. I asked to speak to Lucy.

'Hullo, Lucy.'

'Oh, Mike, really –'

'Lucy, that man's there again.'

'I know, Mike.'

'It's two o'clock in the morning.'

'Two o'clock in the morning. I'm sorry, Mike.' Her voice was so gentle that I said:

'Stop trying not to hurt me.'

'I think I'd better ring off.'

'I'll ring off, damn it.'

I stood by the telephone, considering, and feeling sick. I felt something between my fingers and looked down at the piece of paper with Nigel's telephone number on it. I lifted the receiver and dialled it.

I waited almost a minute and then a woman's voice said: 'Yes? Who is that please?'

I think I said: 'I want to know what's going on.'

The woman said quickly: 'Who is that speaking? You haf the wrong number.'

'I do not,' I retaliated briskly. 'Please bring Nigel to the phone.'

'Nigel is in the Chair. You are interrupting our meeting with this demand. There is much on the agenda. I cannot attend to you, sir.'

'This is the Ministry of Pensions,' I said, and I heard the woman breathing laboriously. Then she cut me off.

I walked back through the party and looked for the front door. I was thinking that everything had been more or less resolved. Margo's grievance had had its airing; she felt the better for it, and all anyone had to do now was to ask Nigel what he was up to and press the point until a satisfactory answer was achieved. As for me, time would heal and time would cure. I knew it, and it was the worst thing of all. I didn't want to be cured. I wanted the madness of my love for Lucy to go on lurching at me from dreams; to mock me from

half-empty glasses; to leap at me unexpectedly. In time
Lucy's face would fade to a pin-point; in time I would
see her on the street and greet her with casualness, and
sit with her over coffee, quietly discussing the flow
beneath the bridges since last we met. Today – not
even that, for already it was tomorrow – would slide
away like all the other days. Not a red-letter day. Not the
day of my desperate bidding. Not the day on which
the love of my life was snaffled away from me. I opened
the front door and looked out into the night. It was
cold and uncomforting. I liked it like that. I hated the
moment, yet I loved it because in it I still loved Lucy.
Deliberately I swung the door and shut away the darkness and drizzle. As I went back to the party the sadness
of all the forgetting stung me. Even already, I thought,
time is at work; time is ticking her away; time is
destroying her, killing all there was between us. And
with time on my side I would look back on the day
without bitterness and without emotion. I would
remember it only as a flash on the brittle surface of
nothing, as a day that was rather funny, as the day we
got drunk on cake.

Lovers of Their Time

Looking back on it, it seemed to have to do with that particular decade in London. Could it have happened, he wondered, at any other time except the 1960s? That feeling was intensified, perhaps, because the whole thing had begun on New Year's Day, 1963, long before that day became a bank holiday in England. 'That'll be two and nine,' she'd said, smiling at him across her counter, handing him toothpaste and emery boards in a bag. 'Colgate's, remember,' his wife had called out as he was leaving the flat. 'The last stuff we had tasted awful.'

His name was Norman Britt. It said so on a small plastic name-plate in front of his position in the travel agency where he worked, Travel-Wide as it was called. *Marie* a badge on her light-blue shop-coat announced. His wife, who worked at home, assembling jewellery for a firm that paid her on a production basis, was called Hilda.

Green's the Chemist's and Travel-Wide were in Vincent Street, a street that was equidistant from Paddington Station and Edgware Road. The flat where Hilda worked all day was in Putney. Marie lived in Reading with her mother and her mother's friend Mrs Druk, both of them widows. She caught the 8.05 every morning to Paddington and usually the 6.30 back.

He was forty in 1963, as Hilda was; Marie was twenty-eight. He was tall and thin, with a David Niven moustache. Hilda was thin also, her dark hair beginning to grey, her sharply featured face pale. Marie was well-covered, carefully made up, her hair dyed blonde. She smiled a lot, a slack, half-crooked smile that made her eyes screw up and twinkle; she exuded laziness and generosity. She and her friend Mavis went dancing a lot in Reading and had a sizeable collection of men friends. 'Fellas' they called them.

Buying things from her now and again in Green's the Chemist's Norman had come to the conclusion that she was of a tartish disposition, and imagined that if ever he sat with her over a drink in the nearby Drummer Boy the occasion could easily lead to a hug on the street afterwards. He imagined her coral-coloured lips, like two tiny sausages, only softer, pressed upon his moustache and his abbreviated mouth. He imagined the warmth of her hand in his. For all that, she was a little outside reality: she was there to desire, to glow erotically in the heady atmosphere of the Drummer Boy, to light cigarettes for in a fantasy.

'Isn't it cold?' he said as she handed him the emery boards and the toothpaste.

'Shocking,' she agreed, and hesitated, clearly wanting to say something else. 'You're in that Travel-Wide,' she added in the end. 'Me and my friend want to go to Spain this year.'

'It's very popular. The Costa Brava?'

'That's right.' She handed him threepence change. 'In May.'

'Not too hot on the Costa in May. If you need any help –'

'Just the bookings.'

'I'd be happy to make them for you. Look in any time. Britt the name is. I'm on the counter.'

'If I may, Mr Britt. I could slip out maybe at four, or roundabout.'

'Today, you mean?'

'We want to fix it up.'

'Naturally. I'll keep an eye out for you.'

It was hard not to call her madam or miss, the way he'd normally do. He had heard himself saying that he'd be happy to make the bookings for her, knowing that that was business jargon, knowing that the unfussy voice he'd used was a business one also. Her friend was a man, he supposed, some snazzy tough in a car. 'See you later then,' he said, but already she was serving another customer, advising about lipstick refills.

She didn't appear in Travel-Wide at four o'clock; she hadn't come when the doors closed at five-thirty. He was aware of a sense of disappointment, combined with one of anticipation: for if she'd come at four, he reflected as he left the travel agency, their bit of business would be in the past rather than the future. She'd look in some other time and he'd just have to trust to luck that if he happened to be busy with another customer she'd be able to wait. There'd be a further occasion, when she called to collect the tickets themselves.

'Ever so sorry,' she said on the street, her voice coming from behind him. 'Couldn't get away, Mr Britt.'

He turned and smiled at her, feeling the movement

of his moustache as he parted his lips. He knew only too well, he said. 'Some other time then?'

'Maybe tomorrow. Maybe lunchtime.'

'I'm off myself from twelve to one. Look, you wouldn't fancy a drink? I could advise you just as easily over a drink.'

'Oh, you wouldn't have the time. No, I mustn't take advantage –'

'You're not at all. If you've got ten minutes?'

'Well, it's awfully good of you, Mr Britt. But I really feel I'm taking advantage, I really do.'

'A New Year's drink.'

He pushed open the doors of the saloon bar of the Drummer Boy, a place he didn't often enter except for office drinks at Christmas or when someone leaving the agency was being given a send-off. Ron Stocks and Mr Blackstaffe were usually there in the evenings: he hoped they'd be there now to see him in the company of the girl from Green's the Chemist's. 'What would you like?' he asked her.

'Gin and peppermint's my poison, only honestly I should pay. No, let me ask you –'

'I wouldn't dream of it. We can sit over there, look.'

The Drummer Boy, so early in the evening, wasn't full. By six o'clock the advertising executives from the firm of Dalton, Dure and Higgins, just round the corner, would have arrived, and the architects from Frine and Knight. Now there was only Mrs Gregan, old and alcoholic, known to everyone, and a man called Bert, with his poodle, Jimmy. It was disappointing that Ron Stocks and Mr Blackstaffe weren't there.

'You were here lunchtime Christmas Eve,' she said.

'Yes, I was.' He paused, placing her gin and pepper-mint on a cardboard mat that advertised Guinness. 'I saw you too.'

He drank some of his Double Diamond and care-fully wiped the traces of foam from his moustache. He realized now that it would, of course, be quite imposs-ible to give her a hug on the street outside. That had been just imagination, wishful thinking as his mother would have said. And yet he knew that when he arrived home twenty-five or so minutes late he would not tell Hilda that he'd been advising an assistant from Green's the Chemist's about a holiday on the Costa Brava. He wouldn't even say he'd been in the Drummer Boy. He'd say Blackstaffe had kept everyone late, going through the new package that Eurotours were offer-ing in Germany and Luxembourg this summer. Hilda wouldn't in a million years suspect that he'd been sit-ting in a public house with a younger woman who was quite an eyeful. As a kind of joke, she quite regularly suggested that his sexual drive left something to be desired.

'We were thinking about the last two weeks in May,' Marie said. 'It's when Mavis can get off too.'

'Mavis?'

'My friend, Mr Britt.'

Hilda was watching *Z-Cars* in the sitting-room, drink-ing V.P. wine. His stuff was in the oven, she told him. 'Thanks,' he said.

Sometimes she was out when he returned in the

evenings. She went round to friends, a Mr and Mrs Fowler, with whom she drank V.P. and played bridge. On other occasions she went to the Club, which was a place with a licence, for card-players and billiard-players. She quite liked her social life, but always said beforehand when she'd be out and always made arrangements about leaving food in the oven. Often in the daytime she'd go and make jewellery with Violet Parkes, who also went in for this occupation; and often Violet Parkes spent the day with Hilda. The jewellery-making consisted for the most part of threading plastic beads on to a string or arranging plastic pieces in the settings provided. Hilda was quick at it and earned more than she would have if she went out every day, saving the fares for a start. She was better at it than Violet Parkes.

'All right then?' she said when he carried his tray of food into the sitting-room and sat down in front of the television set. 'Want some V.P., eh?'

Her eyes continued to watch the figures on the screen as she spoke. He knew she'd prefer to be in the Fowlers' house or at the Club, although now that they'd acquired a TV set the evenings passed easier when they were alone together.

'No, thanks,' he said in reply to her offer of wine and he began to eat something that appeared to be a rissole. There were two of them, round and brown in a tin-foil container that also contained gravy. He hoped she wasn't going to be demanding in their bedroom. He eyed her, for sometimes he could tell.

'Hi,' she said, noticing the glance. 'Feeling fruity,

dear?' She laughed and winked, her suggestive voice seeming odd as it issued from her thin, rather dried-up face. She was always saying things like that, for no reason that Norman could see, always talking about feeling fruity or saying she could see he was keen when he wasn't in the least. Norman considered that she was unduly demanding and often wondered what it would be like to be married to someone who was not. Now and again, fatigued after the intensity of her love-making, he lay staring at the darkness, wondering if her bedroom appetites were related in some way to the fact that she was unable to bear children, if her abandon reflected a maternal frustration. Earlier in their married life she'd gone out every day to an office where she'd been a filing clerk; in the evenings they'd often gone to the cinema.

He lay that night, after she'd gone to sleep, listening to her heavy breathing, thinking of the girl in Green's the Chemist's. He went through the whole day in his mind, seeing himself leaving the flat in Putney, hearing Hilda calling out about the emery boards and the toothpaste, seeing himself reading the *Daily Telegraph* in the Tube. Slowly he went through the morning, deliciously anticipating the moment when she handed him his change. With her smile mistily hovering, he recalled the questions and demands of a number of the morning's customers. 'Fix us up Newcastle and back?' a couple inquired. 'Mid-week's cheaper, is it?' A man with a squashed-up face wanted a week in Holland for himself and his sister and his sister's husband. A woman asked about Greece, another about cruises on the Nile, a third about the Scilly Isles. Then he placed the Closed sign in front of his position at the counter and went out to have lunch in Bette's Sandwiches off the Edgware Road. 'Packet of emery boards,' he said again in Green's the Chemist's, 'and a small Colgate's.' After that there was the conversation they'd had, and then the afternoon with her smile still mistily hovering, as in fact it had, and then her presence beside him in the Drummer Boy. Endlessly she lifted the glass of gin and peppermint to her lips, endlessly she smiled. When he slept he dreamed of her. They were walking in Hyde Park and her shoe fell off. 'I could tell you were a deep one,' she said, and the next thing was Hilda was having one of her early-morning appetites.

'I don't know what it is about that chap,' Marie confided to Mavis. 'Something, though.'

'Married, is he?'

'Oh, he would be, chap like that.'

'Now, you be careful, girl.'

'He has Sinatra's eyes. That blue, you know.'

'Now, Marie –'

'I like an older fella. He's got a nice moustache.'

'So's that fella in the International.'

'Wet behind the ears. And my God, his dandruff!'

They left the train together and parted on the platform, Marie making for the Underground, Mavis hurrying for a bus. It was quite convenient, really, living in Reading and travelling to Paddington every day. It was only half an hour and chatting on the journey passed the time. They didn't travel back together in the evenings because Mavis nearly always did an hour's overtime. She was a computer programmer.

'I talked to Mavis. It's OK about the insurance,' Marie said in Travel-Wide at half past eleven that morning, having slipped out when the shop seemed slack. There'd been some details about insurance which he'd raised the evening before. He always advised insurance, but he'd quite understood when she'd made the point that she'd better discuss the matter with her friend before committing herself to the extra expenditure.

'So I'll go ahead and book you,' he said. 'There'll just be the deposit.'

Marie wrote the cheque. She pushed the pink slip across the counter to him. 'Payable to Travel-Wide.'

'That's quite correct.' He glanced at it and wrote her a receipt. He said:

'I looked out another brochure or two. I'd quite like to go through them with you. So you can explain what's what to your friend.'

'Oh, that's very nice, Mr Britt. But I got to get back. I mean, I shouldn't be out in the middle of the morning.'

'Any chance of lunchtime?'

His suavity astounded him. He thought of Hilda, deftly working at her jewellery, stringing orange and yellow beads, listening to the Jimmy Young programme.

'Lunchtime, Mr Britt?'

'We'd maybe talk about the brochures.'

He fancied her, she said to herself. He was making a pass, talking about brochures and lunchtime. Well, she wasn't disagreeable. She'd meant what she'd said to Mavis: she liked an older fella and she liked his moustache, so smooth it looked as if he put something on it. She liked the name Norman.

'All right then,' she said.

He couldn't suggest Bette's Sandwiches because you stood up at a shelf on the wall and ate the sandwiches off a cardboard plate.

'We could go to the Drummer Boy,' he suggested instead. 'I'm off at twelve-fifteen.'

'Say half past, Mr Britt.'

'I'll be there with the brochures.'

Again he thought of Hilda. He thought of her wiry, pasty limbs and the way she had of snorting. Sometimes when they were watching the television she'd suddenly want to sit on his knee. She'd get worse as she grew older; she'd get scrawnier; her hair, already coarse, would get dry and grey. He enjoyed the evenings when she went out to the Club or to her friends the Fowlers. And yet he wasn't being fair because in very many ways she did her best. It was just that you didn't always feel like having someone on your knee after a day's work.

'Same?' he said in the Drummer Boy.

'Yes please, Mr Britt.' She'd meant to say that the drinks were definitely on her, after what he'd spent last night. But in her flurry she forgot. She picked up the brochures he'd left on the seat beside her. She pretended to read one, but all the time she was watching him as he stood by the bar. He smiled as he turned and came back with their drinks. He said something about it being a nice way to do business. He was drinking gin and peppermint himself.

'I meant to pay for the drinks. I meant to say I would. I'm sorry, Mr Britt.'

'Norman my name is.' He surprised himself again by the ease with which he was managing the situation. They'd have their drinks and then he'd suggest some of the shepherd's pie, or a ham-and-salad roll if she'd prefer it. He'd buy her another gin and peppermint to get her going. Eighteen years ago he used to buy Hilda further glasses of V.P. wine with the same thought in mind.

They finished with the brochures. She told him she lived in Reading; she talked about the town. She mentioned her mother and her mother's friend Mrs Druk, who lived with them, and Mavis. She told him a lot about Mavis. No man was mentioned, no boyfriend or fiancé.

'Honestly,' she said, 'I'm not hungry.' She couldn't have touched a thing. She just wanted to go on drinking gin with him. She wanted to get slightly squiffy, a thing she'd never done before in the middle of the day. She wanted to put her arm through his.

'It's been nice meeting you,' he said.

'A bit of luck.'

'I think so too, Marie.' He ran his forefinger between the bones on the back of her hand, so gently that it made her want to shiver. She didn't take her hand away, and when she continued not to he took her hand in his.

*

After that they had lunch together every day, always in the Drummer Boy. People saw them, Ron Stocks and Mr Blackstaffe from Travel-Wide, Mr Fineman, the pharmacist from Green's the Chemist's. Other people from the travel agency and from the chemist's saw them walking about the streets, usually hand in hand. They would look together into the shop windows of Edgware Road, drawn particularly to an antique shop full of brass. In the evenings he would walk with her to Paddington Station and have a drink in one of the bars. They'd embrace on the platform, as other people did.

Mavis continued to disapprove; Marie's mother and Mrs Druk remained ignorant of the affair. The holiday on the Costa Brava that May was not a success because all the time Marie kept wishing Norman Britt was with her. Occasionally, while Mavis read magazines on the beach, Marie wept and Mavis pretended not to notice. She was furious because Marie's low spirits meant that it was impossible for them to get to know fellas. For months they'd been looking forward to the holiday and now, just because of a clerk in a travel agency, it was a flop. 'I'm sorry, dear,' Marie kept saying, trying to smile; but when they returned to London the friendship declined. 'You're making a fool of yourself,' Mavis pronounced harshly, 'and it's dead boring having to hear about it.' After that they ceased to travel together in the mornings.

The affair remained unconsummated. In the hour and a quarter allotted to each of them for lunch there was nowhere they might have gone to let their passion for one another run its course. Everywhere was public: Travel-Wide and the chemist's shop, the Drummer Boy, the streets they walked. Neither could easily spend a night away from home. Her mother and Mrs Druk would guess that something untoward was in the air; Hilda, deprived of her bedroom mating, would no longer be nonchalant in front of the TV. It would all come out if they were rash, and they sensed some danger in that.

'Oh, darling,' she whispered one October evening at Paddington, huddling herself against him. It was foggy and cold. The fog was in her pale hair, tiny droplets that only he, being close to her, could see. People hurried through the lit-up station, weary faces anxious to be home.

'I know,' he said, feeling as inadequate as he always did at the station.

'I lie awake and think of you,' she whispered.

'You've made me live,' he whispered back.

'And you me. Oh, God, and you me.' She was gone before she finished speaking, swinging into the train as it moved away, her bulky red handbag the last thing he saw. It would be eighteen hours before they'd meet again.

He turned his back on her train and slowly made his way through the crowds, his reluctance to start the journey back to the flat in Putney seeming physical, like a pain, inside him. 'Oh, for God's sake!' a woman cried angrily at him, for he had been in her way and had moved in the same direction as she had in seeking to avoid her, causing a second collision. She dropped magazines on to the platform and he helped her to pick them up, vainly apologizing.

It was then, walking away from this woman, that he saw the sign. *Hotel Entrance* it said in red neon letters, beyond the station's main bookstall. It was the back of the Great Western Royal, a short-cut to its comforts for train travellers at the end of their journey. If only, he thought, they could share a room there. If only for one single night they were granted the privilege of being man and wife. People passed through the swing-doors beneath the glowing red sign, people hurrying, with newspapers or suitcases. Without quite knowing why, he passed through the swing-doors himself.

He walked up two brief flights of steps, through another set of doors, and paused in the enormous hall of the Great Western Royal Hotel. Ahead of him, to the left, was the long, curved reception counter and, to the right, the porter's desk. Small tables and armchairs were everywhere; it was carpeted underfoot. There were signs to lifts and to the bar and the restaurant. The stairway, gently rising to his left, was gracious, carpeted also.

They would sit for a moment in this hall, he imagined, as other people were sitting now, a few with drinks, others with pots of tea and plates half empty of assorted biscuits. He stood for a moment, watching these people, and then, as though he possessed a room in the hotel, he mounted the stairs, saying to himself that it must somehow be possible, that surely they could share a single night in the splendour of this place. There was a landing, made into a lounge, with armchairs and tables, as in the hall below. People conversed quietly; a foreign waiter, elderly and limping, collected silver-plated teapots; a Pekinese dog slept on a woman's lap.

The floor above was different. It was a long, wide corridor with bedroom doors on either side of it. Other corridors, exactly similar, led off it. Chambermaids passed him with lowered eyes; someone gently laughed in a room marked *Staff Only*; a waiter wheeled a trolley containing covered dishes, and a bottle of wine wrapped in a napkin. *Bathroom* a sign said, and he looked in, just to see what a bathroom in the Great Western Royal Hotel would be like. 'My God!' he whispered, possessed immediately with the idea that was, for him, to make the decade of the 1960s different. Looking back on it, he was for ever after unable to recall the first moment he beheld the bathroom on the second floor without experiencing the shiver of pleasure he'd experienced at the time. Slowly he entered. He locked the door and slowly sat down on the edge of the bath. The place was huge, as the bath itself was, like somewhere in a palace. The walls were marble, white veined delicately with grey. Two monstrous brass taps, the biggest bath taps he'd ever in his life seen, seemed to know already that he and Marie would come to the bathroom. They seemed almost to wink an invitation to him, to tell him that the bathroom was a comfortable place and not often in use since private bathrooms were now attached to most of the bedrooms. Sitting in his mackintosh coat on the edge of the bath, he wondered what Hilda would say if she could see him now.

He suggested it to Marie in the Drummer Boy. He led up to it slowly, describing the interior of the Great Western Royal Hotel and how he had wandered about it because he hadn't wanted to go home. 'Actually,' he said, 'I ended up in a bathroom.'

'You mean the toilet, dear? Taken short –'

'No, not the toilet. A bathroom on the second floor. Done out in marble, as a matter of fact.'

She replied that honestly he was a one, to go into a bathroom like that when he wasn't even staying in the place! He said:

'What I mean, Marie, it's somewhere we could go.'

'Go, dear?'

'It's empty half the time. Nearly all the time it must be. I mean, we could be there now. This minute if we wanted to.'

'But we're having our lunch, Norman.'

'That's what I mean. We could even be having it there.'

From the saloon bar's juke-box a lugubrious voice pleaded for a hand to be held. *Take my hand*, sang Elvis Presley, *take my whole life too*. The advertising executives from Dalton, Dure and Higgins were loudly talking about their hopes of gaining the Canadian Pacific account. Less noisily the architects from Frine and Knight complained about local planning regulations.

'In a bathroom, Norman? But we couldn't just go into a bathroom.'

'Why not?'

'Well, we couldn't. I mean, we *couldn't*.'

'What I'm saying is we could.'

'I want to marry you, Norman. I want us to be together. I don't want just going to a bathroom in some hotel.'

'I know; I want to marry you too. But we've got to work it out. You know we've got to work it out, Marie – getting married.'

'Yes, I know.'

It was a familiar topic of conversation between them. They took it for granted that one day, somehow, they would be married. They had talked about Hilda. He'd described Hilda to her, he'd drawn a picture in Marie's mind of Hilda bent over her jewellery-making in a Putney flat, or going out to drink V.P. with the Fowlers or at the Club. He hadn't presented a flattering picture of his wife, and when Marie had quite timidly said that she didn't much care for the sound of her he had agreed that naturally she wouldn't. The only aspect of Hilda he didn't touch upon was her bedroom appetite, night starvation as he privately dubbed it. He didn't mention it because he guessed it might be upsetting.

What they had to work out where Hilda was concerned were the economics of the matter. He would never, at Travel-Wide or anywhere else, earn a great deal of money. Familiar with Hilda's nature, he knew that as soon as a divorce was mooted she'd set out to claim as much alimony as she possibly could, which by law he would have to pay. She would state that she only made jewellery for pin-money and increasingly found it difficult to do so due to a developing tendency towards chilblains or arthritis, anything she could think of. She would hate him for rejecting her, for depriving her of a tame companion. Her own resentment at not being able to have children would somehow latch on to his unfaithfulness: she would see a pattern which wasn't really there, bitterness would come into her eyes.

Marie had said that she wanted to give him the children he had never had. She wanted to have children at once and she knew she could. He knew it too: having children was part of her, you'd only to look at her. Yet that would mean she'd have to give up her job, which she wanted to do when she married anyway, which in turn would mean that all three of them would have to subsist on his meagre salary. And not just all three, the children also.

It was a riddle that mocked him: he could find no answer, and yet he believed that the more he and Marie were together, the more they talked to one another and continued to be in love, the more chance there was of suddenly hitting upon a solution. Not that Marie always listened when he went on about it. She agreed they had to solve their problem, but now and again just pretended it wasn't there. She liked to forget about the existence of Hilda. For an hour or so when she was with him she liked to assume that quite soon, in July or even June, they'd be married. He always brought her back to earth.

'Look, let's just have a drink in the hotel,' he urged. 'Tonight, before the train. Instead of having one in the buffet.'

'But it's a hotel, Norman. I mean, it's for people to stay in –'

'Anyone can go into a hotel for a drink.'

That evening, after their drink in the hotel bar, he led her to the first-floor landing that was also a lounge. It was warm in the hotel. She said she'd like to sink down into one of the armchairs and fall asleep. He laughed at that; he didn't suggest an excursion to the bathroom, sensing that he shouldn't rush things. He saw her on to her train, abandoning her to her mother and Mrs Druk and Mavis. He knew that all during the journey she would be mulling over the splendours of the Great Western Royal.

December came. It was no longer foggy, but the weather was colder, with an icy wind. Every evening, before her train, they had their drink in the hotel. 'I'd love to show you that bathroom,' he said once. 'Just for fun.' He hadn't been pressing it in the least; it was the first time he'd mentioned the bathroom since he'd mentioned it originally. She giggled and said he was terrible. She said she'd miss her train if she went looking at bathrooms, but he said there'd easily be time. 'Gosh!' she whispered, standing in the doorway, looking in. He put his arm around her shoulders and drew her inside, fearful in case a chambermaid should see them loitering there. He locked the door and kissed her. In almost twelve months it was their first embrace in private.

They went to the bathroom during the lunch hour on New Year's Day, and he felt it was right that they should celebrate in this way the anniversary of their first real meeting. His early impression of her, that she was of a tartish disposition, had long since been dispelled. Voluptuous she might seem to the eye, but beneath that misleading surface she was prim and proper. It was odd that Hilda, who looked dried-up and wholly uninterested in the sensual life, should also belie her appearance. 'I've never done it before,' Marie confessed in the bathroom, and he loved her the more for that. He loved her simplicity in this matter, her desire to remain a virgin until her wedding. But since she repeatedly swore that she could marry no one else, their anticipating of their wedding-night did not matter. 'Oh, God, I love you,' she whispered, naked for the first time in the bathroom. 'Oh, Norman, you're so good to me.'

After that it became a regular thing. He would saunter from the hotel bar, across the huge entrance lounge, and take a lift to the second floor. Five minutes later she would follow, with a towel brought specially from Reading in her handbag. In the bathroom they always whispered, and would sit together in a warm bath after their love-making, still murmuring about the future, holding hands beneath the surface of the water. No one ever rapped on the door to ask what was going on in there. No one ever questioned them as they returned, separately, to the bar, with the towel they'd shared damping her compact and her handkerchief.

Years instead of months began to go by. On the juke-box in the Drummer Boy the voice of Elvis Presley was no longer heard. '*Why she had to go I don't know,*' sang the Beatles, '*she didn't say . . . I believe in yesterday.'* And Eleanor Rigby entered people's lives, and Sergeant Pepper with her. The fantasies of secret agents, more fantastic than ever before, filled the screens of London's cinemas. Carnaby Street, like a jolly trash-can, overflowed with noise and colour. And in the bathroom of the Great Western Royal Hotel the love affair of Norman Britt and Marie was touched with the same preposterousness. They ate sandwiches in the bathroom; they drank wine. He whispered to her of the faraway places he knew about but had never been to: the Bahamas, Brazil, Peru, Seville at Easter, the Greek islands, the Nile, Shiraz, Persepolis, the Rocky Mountains. They should have been saving their money, not spending it on gin and peppermint in the bar of the hotel and in the Drummer Boy. They should have been racking their brains to find a solution to the problem of Hilda, but it was nicer to pretend that one day they would walk together in Venice or Tuscany. It was all so different from the activities that began with Hilda's bedroom appetites, and it was different from the coarseness that invariably surfaced when Mr Black-staffe got going in the Drummer Boy on an evening when a Travel-Wide employee was being given a send-off. Mr Blackstaffe's great joke on such occasions was that he liked to have sexual intercourse with his wife at night and that she preferred the conjunction in the mornings. He was always going on about how difficult it was in the mornings, what with the children liable to interrupt you, and he usually went into details about certain other, more intimate preferences of his wife's. He had a powerful, waxy guffaw, which he brought regularly into play when he was engaged in this kind of conversation, allying it with a nudging motion of the elbow. Once his wife actually turned up in the Drummer Boy and Norman found it embarrassing even to look at her, knowing as he did so much about her private life. She was a stout middle-aged woman with decorated spectacles: her appearance, too, apparently belied much.

In the bathroom all such considerations, disliked equally by Norman Britt and Marie, were left behind. Romance ruled their brief sojourns, and love sanctified – or so they believed – the passion of their physical intimacy. Love excused their eccentricity, for only love could have found in them a willingness to engage in the deception of a hotel and the courage that went with it: that they believed most of all.

But afterwards, selling tickets to other people or putting Marie on her evening train, Norman sometimes felt depressed. And then gradually, as more time passed, the depression increased and intensified. 'I'm so sad,' he whispered in the bathroom once, 'when I'm not with you. I don't think I can stand it.' She dried herself on the towel brought specially from Reading in her large red handbag. 'You'll have to tell her,' she said, with an edge in her voice that hadn't ever been there before. 'I don't want to leave having babies too late.' She wasn't twenty-eight any more; she was thirty-one. 'I mean, it isn't fair on me,' she said.

He knew it wasn't fair on her, but going over the whole thing yet again in Travel-Wide that afternoon he also knew that poverty would destroy them. He'd never earn much more than he earned now. The babies Marie wanted, and which he wanted too, would soak up what there was like blotting-paper; they'd probably have to look for council accommodation. It made him weary to think about it, it gave him a headache. But he knew she was right: they couldn't go on for ever, living off a passing idyll, in the bathroom of a hotel. He even thought, quite seriously for a moment, of causing Hilda's death.

Instead he told her the truth, one Thursday evening after she'd been watching *The Avengers* on television. He just told her he'd met someone, a girl called Marie, he said, whom he had fallen in love with and wished to marry. 'I was hoping we could have a divorce,' he said.

Hilda turned the sound on the television set down without in any way dimming the picture, which she continued to watch. Her face did not register the hatred he had imagined in it when he rejected her; nor did bitterness suddenly enter her eyes. Instead she shook her head at him, and poured herself some more V.P. She said:

'You've gone barmy, Norman.'

'You can think that if you like.'

'Wherever'd you meet a girl, for God's sake?'

'At work. She's there in Vincent Street. In a shop.'

'And what's she think of you, may I ask?'

'She's in love with me, Hilda.'

She laughed. She told him to pull the other one, adding that it had bells on it.

'Hilda, I'm not making this up. I'm telling you the truth.'

She smiled into her V.P. She watched the screen for a moment, then she said:

'And how long's this charming stuff been going on, may I inquire?'

He didn't want to say for years. Vaguely, he said it had been going on for just a while.

'You're out of your tiny, Norman. Just because you fancy some piece in a shop doesn't mean you go getting hot under the collar. You're no tomcat, you know, old boy.'

'I didn't say I was.'

'You're no sexual mechanic.'

'Hilda –'

'All chaps fancy things in shops: didn't your mother tell you that? D'you think I haven't fancied stuff myself, the chap who came to do the blinds, that randy little postman with his rugby songs?'

'I'm telling you I want a divorce, Hilda.'

She laughed. She drank more V.P. wine. 'You're up a gum tree,' she said, and laughed again.

'Hilda –'

'Oh, for God's sake!' All of a sudden she was angry, but more, he felt, because he was going on, not because of what he was actually demanding. She thought him ridiculous and said so. And then she added all the things he'd thought himself: that people like them didn't get divorces, that unless his girlfriend was well-heeled the whole thing would be a sheer bloody nonsense, with bloody solicitors the only ones to benefit. 'They'll send you to the cleaners, your bloody solicitors will,' she loudly pointed out, anger still trembling in her voice. 'You'd be paying them back for years.'

'I don't care,' he began, although he did. 'I don't care about anything except –'

'Of course you do, you damn fool.'

'Hilda –'

'Look, get over her. Take her into a park after dark or something. It'll make no odds to you and me.'

She turned the sound on the television up and quite quickly finished the V.P. wine. Afterwards, in their bedroom, she turned to him with an excitement that was greater than usual. 'God, that switched me on,' she whispered in the darkness, gripping him with her limbs. 'The stuff we were talking about, that girl.' When she'd finished her love-making she said, 'I had it with that postman, you know. Swear to God. In the kitchen. And since we're on the subject, Fowler looks in here the odd time.'

He lay beside her in silence, not knowing whether or not to believe what she was saying. It seemed at first that she was keeping her end up because he'd mentioned Marie, but then he wasn't so sure. 'We had a foursome once,' she said, 'the Fowlers and me and a chap that used to be in the Club.'

She began to stroke his face with her fingers, the way he hated. She always seemed to think that if she stroked his face it would excite him. She said, 'Tell me more about this piece you fancy.'

He told her to keep her quiet and to make her stop stroking his face. It didn't seem to matter now if he told her how long it had been going on, not since she'd made her revelations about Fowler and the postman. He even enjoyed telling her, about the New Year's Day when he'd bought the emery boards and the Colgate's, and how he'd got to know Marie because she and Mavis were booking a holiday on the Costa Brava.

'But you've never actually?'

'Yes, we have.'

'For God's sake where? Doorways or something? In the park?'

'We go to a hotel.'

'You old devil!'

'Listen, Hilda –'

'For God's sake go on, love. Tell me about it.'

He told her about the bathroom and she kept asking him questions, making him tell her details, asking him to describe Marie to her. Dawn was breaking when they finished talking.

'Forget about the divorce stuff,' she said quite casually at breakfast. 'I wouldn't want to hear no more of that. I wouldn't want you ruined for my sake, dear.'

He didn't want to see Marie that day, although he had to because it was arranged. In any case she knew he'd been going to tell his wife the night before; she'd want to hear the outcome.

'Well?' she said in the Drummer Boy.

He shrugged. He shook his head. He said:

'I told her.'

'And what'd she say, Norman? What'd Hilda say?'

'She said I was barmy to be talking about divorce.

She said what I said to you: that we wouldn't manage with the alimony.'

They sat in silence. Eventually Marie said:

'Then can't you leave her? Can't you just not go back? We could get a flat somewhere. We could put off kiddies, darling. Just walk out, couldn't you?'

'They'd find us. They'd make me pay.'

'We could try it. If I keep on working you could pay what they want.'

'It'll never pan out, Marie.'

'Oh, darling, just walk away from her.'

Which is what, to Hilda's astonishment, he did. One evening when she was at the Club he packed his clothes and went to two rooms in Kilburn that he and Marie had found. He didn't tell Hilda where he was going. He just left a note to say he wouldn't be back.

They lived as man and wife in Kilburn, sharing a lavatory and a bathroom with fifteen other people. In time he received a court summons, and in court was informed that he had behaved meanly and despicably to the woman he'd married. He agreed to pay regular maintenance.

The two rooms in Kilburn were dirty and uncomfortable, and life in them was rather different from the life they had known together in the Drummer Boy and the Great Western Royal Hotel. They planned to find somewhere better, but at a reasonable price that wasn't easy to find. A certain melancholy descended on them, for although they were together they seemed as far away as ever from their own small house, their children and their ordinary contentment.

'We could go to Reading,' Marie suggested.

'Reading?'

'To my mum's.'

'But your mum's nearly disowned you. Your mum's livid, you said yourself she was.'

'People come round.'

She was right. One Sunday afternoon they made the journey to Reading to have tea with Marie's mother and her friend Mrs Druk. Neither of these women addressed Norman, and once when he and Marie were in the kitchen he heard Mrs Druk saying it disgusted her, that he was old enough to be Marie's father. 'Don't think much of him,' Marie's mother replied. 'Pipsqueak really.'

Nevertheless, Marie's mother had missed her daughter's contribution to the household finances and before they returned to London that evening it was arranged that Norman and Marie should move in within a month, on the firm understanding that the very second it was feasible their marriage would take place. 'He's a boarder, mind,' Marie's mother warned. 'Nothing but a boarder in this house.' There were neighbours, Mrs Druk added, to be thought of.

Reading was worse than the two rooms in Kilburn. Marie's mother continued to make disparaging remarks about Norman, about the way he left the lavatory, or the thump of his feet on the stair-carpet, or his fingermarks around the light-switches. Marie would deny these accusations and then there'd be a row, with Mrs Druk joining in because she loved a row, and Marie's mother weeping and then Marie weeping.

Norman had been to see a solicitor about divorcing Hilda, quoting her unfaithfulness with a postman and with Fowler. 'You have your evidence, Mr Britt?' the solicitor inquired, and pursed his lips when Norman said he hadn't.

He knew it was all going to be too difficult. He knew his instinct had been right: he shouldn't have told Hilda, he shouldn't have just walked out. The whole thing had always been unfair on Marie; it had to be when a girl got mixed up with a married man. 'Should think of things like that,' her mother had a way of saying loudly when he was passing an open door. 'Selfish type he is,' Mrs Druk would loudly add.

Marie argued when he said none of it was going to work. But she wasn't as broken-hearted as she might have been a year or so ago, for the strain had told on Marie too, especially the strain in Reading. She naturally wept when Norman said they'd been defeated, and so for a moment did he. He asked for a transfer to another branch of Travel-Wide and was sent to Ealing, far away from the Great Western Royal Hotel.

Eighteen months later Marie married a man in a brewery. Hilda, hearing on some grapevine that Norman was on his own, wrote to him and suggested that bygones should be allowed to be bygones. Lonely in a bed-sitting-room in Ealing, he agreed to talk the situation over with her and after that he agreed to return to their flat. 'No hard feelings,' Hilda said, 'and no deception: there's been a chap from the Club in here, the Woolworth's manager.' No hard feelings, he agreed.

For Norman Britt, as the decade of the 1960s passed, it trailed behind it the marvels of his love affair with Marie. Hilda's scorn when he had confessed had not devalued them, nor had the two dirty rooms in Kilburn, nor the equally unpleasant experience in Reading. Their walk to the Great Western Royal, the drinks they could not afford in the hotel bar, their studied nonchalance as they made their way separately upstairs, seemed to Norman to be a fantasy that had miraculously become real. The second-floor bathroom belonged in it perfectly, the bathroom full of whispers and caressing, where the faraway places of his daily work acquired a hint of magic when he spoke of them to a girl as voluptuous as any of James Bond's. Sometimes on the Tube he would close his eyes and with the greatest pleasure that remained to him he would recall the delicately veined marble and the great brass taps, and the bath that was big enough for two. And now and again he heard what appeared to be the strum of distant music, and the voices of the Beatles celebrating a bathroom love, as they had celebrated Eleanor Rigby and other people of that time.

Bodily Secrets

At fifty-nine, she was on her own, the widow of the O'Neill who had inherited the town's coal business, who had started, as an enterprise of his own, the toy factory. Her children had flown the nest, her parents and her parents-in-law were no longer alive. Her husband had been in his lifetime a smallish though heavily built man, with wide shoulders and an unrelenting, cropped head, like a battering wedge. His cautious eyes had been set well apart beneath woolly eyebrows; small veins had reddened his nose. He had died at the age of sixty-three, falling down in the big, airy hall of Arcangelo House and afterwards not regaining any real awareness of who he was or what had happened. He had built Arcangelo House after he and his wife had stayed in an Italian hotel of that name when they visited Rome on the occasion of Holy Year.

A beauty once, she was a handsome woman still, tall and imposing in her middle age, with a well-covered look that reflected her liking for sweet things. Her grey hair was shaded towards its original brown, and discreetly burnished; she bought clothes extravagantly. She made up her face with precision, taking her time over it; and attended similarly to her fingernails and, in season, her toenails. She had borne four children in all, two of her three daughters being married now, one

51

in Dublin, the other in Trim; the third was a nurse in Philadelphia. Her son, married also, ran the coal business but was more interested in developing a thousand acres of turf-bog he had bought and which he saw as the beginning of an enterprise that he believed would in time outstrip his father's and his grandfather's already established empire. He had inherited their entrepreneur's spirit, and since he'd first been aware of the role laid down for him he had seen himself as their rival. He was married to Thelma, daughter of a Portarlington publican, a girl whom Mrs O'Neill did not care for, considering her common. Particularly she did not care for the thought that one day Thelma would take her own place in Arcangelo House.

From the garden and the upstairs windows the house offered, over fields, a view of the town that was interrupted only by the toy factory. When the wind blew from the south it carried sounds rendered faint over the distance: the cries of children, a car being started somewhere, the saws in the timber works, the grind of a heavy lorry on Daly's Hill. And no matter where the wind came from there was always the bell at the convent, and the bell of Our Lady in Glory, and the Protestant bell on Sundays. At night the street lights and the lights of houses were spread out prettily – the town seen at its best, as Mrs O'Neill often reflected. But increasingly in the vacuum that Arcangelo House had become she reflected also that she felt like a pebble in a drum, and said as much to her bridge companions. They urged her to sell it and build a bungalow, but privately she felt that a bungalow was not her style.

When her husband had died Mrs O'Neill had been fifty-six, and although they had regularly disagreed in their thirty-seven years of marriage they had more often been affectionate companions. They had shared two interests in particular: golf and their children. Together they had attended the occasional race-meeting; and while her husband had not played bridge, she in turn had not inclined to join him in the bar of the Commercial Hotel, where he liked to spend an evening or two a week. Every summer they went to Lahinch or Bundoran for the golf, and for several years after Holy Year they had returned to Rome, to the hotel which had given their house its character and its name. Often, on a night which wasn't a bridge night, Mrs O'Neill wondered about the future and whether she should indeed sell Arcangelo House. When the television came to an end she sat alone in the big open drawing-room, feeling just a little lonely and vaguely wishing that there was another interest in her life besides bridge and golf and her grown-up family. Time had dulled the loss that widowhood had brought, but in no way had it filled the vacuum that was somehow more apparent as time progressed. Once she'd been the centre of things in Arcangelo House, looking after everyone, in charge of other people's lives. 'Ah, come on now,' she'd said a thousand times to the husband who'd died on her. 'You're as big a baby as any of them.' In her days as a beauty she had more or less designed the house herself, standing over MacGuire the architect and endeavouring to picture for him a cool, well-organized hotel in Rome. It still pleased her that she had succeeded so well, not that Arcangelo House was to everyone's taste, she was well aware of that: it was too different, too modern, in a way too grand. But old Canon Kenny, the most educated man for miles about, said he would wager money that the house was the most interesting to be found outside Dublin. It had been featured in *Social and Personal* and MacGuire, who was inordinately proud of it, had asked if a German architect, on a motoring holiday, might come and see it. How could she just leave it all? The garden, once little better than waste-land, had gorgeously matured. The portico, with its clean white arches, was rich with different clematis from June to August. The patio was warm enough to have breakfast on in March. Yet the accomplishing of what she'd wanted in the house and in the garden belonged to the time when she'd been in charge, and was a reminder that nothing now was changing or taking shape due to her efforts.

Occasionally, pursuing such lines of thought, she wondered if she would marry again. She couldn't help herself; she had no desire to remarry, yet widows did so, it was something that quite often occurred. At the golf club there was Sweetman, a few years younger than herself, a bachelor all his life, pleasantly sociable but bleary when he had drink taken, and according to Dolores Fitzfynne a tightwad. There was Corkin, who was her own age, but it was hard to think of Corkin without thinking also of the Mrs Corkin there had been, a drear of a woman who had played neither golf nor bridge, who hadn't even had children: Corkin had been infected by her dreariness or else had infected her in the first place. There was no one else, except perhaps Agnew, with his sallow face and his hands, which were sallow also, gesturing in the air, and his faintly high-pitched voice. He was younger than the others, younger than she was herself by seven or eight years, yet she often thought of him in this connection. She thought about him in a different way on the morning her son, Cathal, decreed that the toy factory would have to go. For seventeen years Agnew had been its manager.

In a blue-and-yellow paisley dressing-gown which she'd had all her married life she sat on the edge of her bed, listening to her son on the telephone saying that the people at the toy factory could easily be absorbed elsewhere, that for a long time now he had systematically been running the business down. The toy factory had been profitable only in the immediate postwar years, unable ultimately to sustain the competition which had so ominously built up: long before his death her husband had threatened that it would sooner or later have to close. It was a tiny concern, the loss would not be great.

'All they're making now are the fox-terriers,' Cathal said on the telephone, referring to wooden dogs on wheels.

'The building?' she said. 'Best to have it down, wouldn't it?'

'I could bale garden peat there. I'm going into that, you know.'

She did not say anything. She did not trust this

dark-faced son she'd given birth to. Ceasing to be a toy factory, the building would be expanded when it became the location for one of his enterprises. There might be noise, even a smell of chemicals. You simply couldn't guess what would come along in order that more money might be made. And why should it matter since only a lone woman lived near by?

'We'll have to see,' she said.

'Ah, of course, of course. No hurry at all.'

She did not ask about Agnew. She could not see him being absorbed into the turf business or the coal business, and in any case Cathal didn't like him. Cathal would have him out on the street while you'd wink.

Cathal had his father's wedge of a head, his forehead and wide-apart, narrow eyes. He was the first of their children to be born, the one who had received most attention because the others were girls. Heir to so much, he had been claimed by a thrusting entrepreneur's world from infancy. The girls, except for Siobhan in Philadelphia, had been more mundanely claimed by men.

She wouldn't have minded any of the others being in Arcangelo House, but Thelma had a greedy way of looking at her, as if she couldn't wait to get into the place. Mrs O'Neill dearly wished that her son hadn't married this girl, but he had and that was that. She sighed as she replaced the receiver, seeing Thelma's slightly puffy face, her nose too small for the rest of it. She sat for a moment longer, endeavouring to release her imagination of that face and in the end succeeding. Then she dressed herself and went down to the toy factory. Agnew was in the inner office, standing by the window, his back to her as she entered.

'Mr Agnew.'

'Ah, Mrs O'Neill. Come in, come in, Mrs O'Neill.' He moved so swiftly in turning to greet her that she was reminded of the assured way he danced the quick-step. He came every December to the Golf Club Dance even though he was not a club member and had once confided to her that he had never played the game. 'Croquet,' he'd confided also. 'I used to be quite snappy at croquet.' He had his own expressions, a way of putting things that sometimes sounded odd. Typical that he should mention an old-fashioned game like croquet.

'I hope you're not busy, Mr Agnew. I'm not disturbing you, am I?'

'Heavens above, why would you be? Won't you take a chair, Mrs O'Neill? A cup of tea now?'

There was always this formality. He offered it and seemed shyly to demand it. Her husband had always used his surname, and so did Cathal; at the Golf Club Dance she'd heard other men call him by his initials, B.J. She couldn't in a million years imagine him addressing her as Norah.

'No, I won't have tea, thank you.'

'A taste of sherry at all? I have a nice sweet little sherry –'

'No, thanks. Really, Mr Agnew.'

He smiled, gently closing a glass-fronted cabinet he had opened in expectation of her accepting his hospitality. He was wearing a brown suit chalked with a pinstripe, and a green silk tie. He said:

'Well, it seems we have come to the end of the road.'

'I know. I'm awfully sorry.'

'Mr O'Neill saw it coming years ago.'

'Yes, I'm afraid he did.'

He smiled again; his voice was unperturbed. 'The first day I came up to Arcangelo House I was terrified out of my wits. D'you remember, Mrs O'Neill? Your husband had an advertisement for the job in the *Irish Times*.'

'It seems an age ago.'

'Doesn't it, though? An age.'

His face had acquired a meditative expression. He drew a packet of cigarettes from a pocket of his jacket and opened it slowly, folding back the silver paper. He advanced a single cigarette by knocking the packet on the surface of his desk. He leaned towards her, offering it. His wrists were slim: she had never noticed his wrists before.

'Thank you, Mr Agnew.'

He leaned across the desk again, holding the flame of a cigarette-lighter to the tip of her cigarette. It gleamed with the dull patina of gold, as slender as a coin.

'No, I don't entirely know what I'll do.' He lit his own cigarette and then held it, dangling, in his long fingers.

'Cathal should have something for you. It was my husband's intention, you know, that everyone at the toy factory should be offered something.'

She wanted to make that clear; she wanted to record

this unequivocal statement in the inner office so that later on, if necessary, she could quote herself to Cathal. She inhaled some smoke and released it luxuriously through her nostrils. She was fond of the occasional cigarette, although she never smoked when she was on her own.

'I'm not so sure I'd entirely fit in, Mrs O'Neill. I don't know anything about selling turf.'

She mentioned coal, which after all was the fuel that had made the O'Neills wealthy. There was still a thriving coal business, the biggest in the county.

He shook his head. His hair, once black, was almost completely grey now. 'I don't think,' he said, 'I'd be at home in coal.'

'Well, I only thought I'd mention it.'

'It's more than kind, Mrs O'Neill.'

'My husband wouldn't have wanted anyone not looked after.'

'Oh, indeed I know it.'

She stared at the lipstick mark on her cigarette and then raised the cigarette to her mouth again. It was awkward because she didn't want to walk out of the factory smoking a cigarette, yet it was too soon to crush it out on the ashtray in front of her.

'If there's any way the family can help, you'll say, Mr Agnew?'

'I suppose I'll go to Dublin.'

The remark was not accompanied by one of his glancing smiles; he gave no sign whatsoever that he'd touched upon a fascinating topic. No one knew why he spent weekends occasionally in Dublin, and a certain curiosity had gathered round the mystery of these visits. There was some secret which he kept, which he had not even confided to her husband in his lifetime. He came back melancholy was all her husband had ever reported, and once or twice with bloodshot eyes, as if he had spent the time drinking.

'Though I'd rather not end up in Dublin,' he added now. 'To tell you the full truth, Mrs O'Neill, it's not a city I entirely care for.'

She bent the remains of her cigarette in half, extinguishing it on the ashtray. She stood up, thinking it odd that he'd said Dublin wasn't somewhere he cared for since he visited it so regularly.

'The toy factory was a favourite of my husband's. It saddened him to see it decline.'

'It had its heyday.'

'Yes, it had its day.'

She went, walking with him from the office, through a shed full of unassembled terriers on wheels. The white cut-out bodies with a brown spot around the tail, the brown heads, the little platforms that carried the wheels, the wheels themselves: all these dislocated parts lay about in stacks, seeming unwanted. No one was working in the shed.

He walked with her through other deserted areas, out on to the gravel forecourt that stretched in a semi-circle around the front of the small factory. A man loaded wired cartons on to a lorry. They were still meeting orders in England, Agnew told her. The paint shop was as active as ever, three girls on full time.

He held his hand out, his sallow features illuminated

by another smile. His palm was cool, his grip gentle. He asked her not to worry about him. He assured her he'd be all right.

There were gusts of laughter in the clubhouse. Dessie Fitzfynne had told a Kerry joke, concerning eight Kerry gardai and a cow. Dolores Fitzfynne, who'd just gone round in eighty-two and wanted to talk about that instead, requested that he shouldn't tell another. Sweetman was talking about horses, arranging something about going to the Curragh. Sweetman loved getting parties together to go racing or to Lansdowne Road, or for a weekend down in Kelly's at Rosslare. Paunchy and rubicund, Flanagan kept saying it was his turn and what did anyone want?

'I heard the factory's winding up,' the solicitor, Butler-Regan, remarked in his rowdy voice and she nodded, suddenly feeling dismal. She had forgotten about the toy factory while she'd been on the golf-course, going round in ninety-one, taking three to get out of the rough at the eighth. She'd been playing with Dessie Fitzfynne, opposing Dolores and Flanagan. They'd been beaten, of course.

It was silly to feel dismal just because the facts of commerce dictated the closure of an unprofitable concern. As both Cathal and Agnew had intimated, the end had been a matter of anticipation for years. Only sentiment had prevented such a decision in the lifetime of her husband.

'Ah well, there you are,' Butler-Regan said noisily. ''Tis better let it go, Norah.'

Flanagan handed her another gin and French even though she hadn't asked for one. Overhearing the reference to the toy factory, he said:

'I hear Agnew's wondering what to do with himself.'

'The bold Agnew!' Butler-Regan laughed. He, too, was paunchy and rubicund. He added, laughing again, shouting through this laughter: 'Oh, Master Agnew'll fall on his feet, I'd say.'

They all liked Agnew even though he was so different. He was an easy companion for half an hour or so if you happened to run into him in the bar of the Commercial Hotel; he was always willing to drop into conversation with you on the street. He had digs with the Misses McShane in a house called St Kevin's, where he was regularly to be seen tending the front garden, behind silver-painted railings set in a low concrete wall. He also walked the Misses McShane's dog, Mandy, about the town, and on Sundays he attended the Protestant church unless he happened to be in Dublin.

'We'd all miss Agnew,' Flanagan said. 'That wild Protestant man.' He laughed, making much the same explosive sound that the solicitor did. Did any of them realize, she wondered, that Agnew's quickstep put them all to shame every December?

'Oh, wild is right,' Butler-Regan agreed. 'Wasn't he in the city again a week ago?'

The two men laughed in unison, the burst of noise causing Rita Flanagan to glance sharply across the bar to ascertain if her husband was already drunk. In dog's-tooth skirt and soft fawn golfing-jacket, Mrs

O'Neill wondered what any of them would think if they knew that, quite involuntarily as she stood there, she had again begun to speculate on the possibility of not remaining for ever the widow she presently was. She sipped her gin and French, not taking part in a conversation about Sweetman's outing to the Curragh. In the same involuntary manner she found herself following a thread of thought that led her back to her wedding-day. The O'Neills had insisted on paying for the reception, since her own family were not well-to-do. Old Canon Kenny – neither old nor a canon then – had conducted the service, assisted by a curate called Colquhoun, who had later left the priesthood. They had gone to Bray for their honeymoon and on their first night in the International Hotel she had been jittery. She hadn't known how it should be, whether she should simply take her clothes off or wait for him to say something, whether or not there was going to be preliminary kissing. She'd gone as red as anything after they'd come up from the restaurant. 'I think that waiter knew,' she'd whispered on the stairs, not noticing there was a maid just behind them. He'd been jittery too, and in the end it was she who inaugurated the kissing and in fact had taken his tie off. What on earth would it be like being in a bedroom in Bray with Agnew? There was fat on her shoulders now, which hadn't been there before, and naturally her thighs and her hips were no longer the same. Her body had been forgotten in that particular way for many years before her husband's death, almost since the birth of Siobhan. They had come to occupy separate bedrooms in Arcangelo House, having reached the decision that Cathal and the three girls were enough. At first, when it was safe to do so, she had visited the other bedroom, but the habit had dwindled and then ceased. Would it be a form of unfaithfulness to resume it in different circumstances now? It wasn't easy to guess how such things stood at fifty-nine.

Corkin, the widower of the woman who'd been a drear, approached her with the usual sorrowful look in his eyes, as if he still mourned the wife who had played neither bridge nor golf. The eyes themselves, lurking in their despondent wateriness behind spectacles, had pinkish rims and were the only feature you noticed in Corkin's flat face, except possibly his teeth, which moved uncomfortably in his jaw when he ate. He was eating now, chewing crisps from a transparent Tayto bag. His hair was like smooth lead; his limbs jutted from his clothes. There was no doubt whatsoever that Corkin, the manager of a butter business, was looking for a housekeeper in the form of a second wife. There was always a nudge or two in the clubhouse when he approached Mrs O'Neill for a chat.

'Ah, didn't I have a terrible round? Did you see me in front of you, Norah? Wasn't I shocking?'

She denied that. She hadn't noticed his misfortunes, she said, which indeed she hadn't. She might have added that the butter manager couldn't be shocking if he tried for the rest of his life.

'I've been meaning to ask you,' he said. 'Would you be interested in a bunch of delphiniums from the garden, Norah?'

She drank more gin and French. She had plenty of delphiniums at Arcangelo House, she replied, though it was very good of him to offer her more.

'Or the asparagus fern? D'you grow that stuff?'

'I grow asparagus all right. Only I eat it before the fern comes.'

'Ah well, why wouldn't you, Norah.'

Sweetman, at the bar, was sweating like an animal. No woman in her senses would want to marry Sweetman. His trouble with perspiration ironically denied his name, and the caginess Dolores Fitzfynne claimed for him would hardly have been easy to live with. He had a tendency towards forgetfulness when his round came up in the clubhouse and, according to Dolores, the parties he organized for race-meetings or Lansdowne Road were done so to his own pecuniary advantage. 'Too mingy with himself to look sideways at a woman,' Dolores had said, and probably she was right. He was a surveyor with the county council; and if he gave you a lift in his car he had a way of mentioning the high price of petrol.

She watched Sweetman while Corkin continued in his tedious manner, offering her marigold plants. It had surprised her when Agnew had said he'd never in his life played golf. She'd thought afterwards that he would probably have been good. He had the look of someone who had been athletic in his time. His dancing suggested ball sense, she didn't know why.

'To tell you the honest truth, I don't much care for marigolds.'

'The wife loved them. Give Mrs Corkin a box of

marigolds and she'd be pricking them out till Kingdom come.'

He wagged his head; she nodded hers. She allowed a silence to develop in the hope that he'd go away. He said eventually:

'D'you ever watch that thing they have, *Dynasty* is it called?'

'I watched it the odd time.'

'Will you tell me this, Norah: where do they get the stories?'

'I suppose they invent them.'

'Isn't America the shocking place though?'

'I have a daughter there.'

'Ah, sure, of course you have.'

At the bar Butler-Regan looked as though he might sing. Very occasionally he did, striking the bar rhythmically with his fist, trying to make people join in. The club secretary, Dr Walsh, had had to speak to him, explaining that it wasn't usual to sing in a golf club, even adding that he didn't think it quite the thing for a solicitor to sing anywhere. But Butler-Regan had done so again, and had again to be warned. It was said that his wife, who like the late Mrs Corkin played neither bridge nor golf, had a terrible time with him.

'Does your girl ever remark on the *Dynasty* thing to you?' Corkin was inquiring. 'I mean, if it might be accurate?'

'Siobhan has never mentioned *Dynasty*.'

'Well, isn't that extraordinary?'

Ten minutes later the drinking in the clubhouse broke up and Mrs O'Neill drove back to Arcangelo

House. She made scrambled egg and watched a film about drug-running on the television. The police of several nations pursued a foursome of gangsters and finally ran the ringleader to earth in Los Angeles. She dozed off, and when she woke up a priest with a Cork accent was talking about the feast of Corpus Christi. She listened to him until he'd finished and then turned the television off.

In her bedroom she did something she had not done for ten years at least: before she slipped into her night-dress she paused in front of the long looking-glass of her wardrobe and surveyed her naked body. It was most certainly no longer her best feature, she said to herself, remembering it when she was a child, standing up in the bath to be dried. She remembered being naked at last in the bedroom of the International Hotel in Bray, and the awkward voluptuousness that had followed. The bearing of four children, her fondness for sweet things, the insidious nips of gin in the clubhouse – in combination they had taken a toll, making clothes as necessary as all that meticulous care with make-up and hair. The first time she'd been pregnant, with Cathal, she had looked at herself in this same looking-glass, assuring herself that the enormous swelling would simply go away, as indeed it had. But nothing would go away now. Flesh hung loosely, marked with pink imprints of straps or elastic. If she slimmed herself to the bone there would be scrawny, empty skin, loops and pockets, hollows as ugly as the bulges. She drew her night-dress over her head and a pattern of pink roses in tight little bunches hid what she preferred not to see, transforming her again into a handsome woman.

Agnew had sensitive skin, yet could not resist the quality of finely woven tweed. He chose the sober colours, the greys and browns and inconspicuous greens. He bought his Donegal tweed in Kevin and Howlin's in Dublin and had the suits made up by a tailor in Rathmines. Because of his sensitive skin he had the trousers lined.

Agnew had never worn these suits to his office in the toy factory, for they did not seem to him to be sufficiently matter-of-fact for business. He wore them at weekends, when he went to church and on Sunday afternoons when he drove out to Rathfarran and walked around the cliffs, ending up in Lynch's Bar down by the strand, where by arrangement he took his Sunday supper. He wore them also on the weekends when he went to Dublin.

He would miss the cliffs and the strand, he reflected at breakfast one morning, a few weeks after his visit from Mrs O'Neill. He would miss the toy factory too, of course, and the people he had come to know in a passing kind of way, without intimacy or closeness but yet agreeably. In the snug, overcrowded dining-room of the terraced house called St Kevin's he broke a piece of toast in half and poured himself more tea. He had been fortunate in St Kevin's, fortunate because he was the only lodger and because the Misses McShane had never sought to share a meal with him, fortunate that the house was clean and the cooking averagely good.

He'd been fortunate that his interest had never flagged in the job at the toy factory. He would take away with him a sample of every single wooden toy that had been manufactured during his time there: the duck with the quivering bill, the kangaroos, the giraffes, the little red steam engines, the donkeys and carts, the bricks, the elephants, the fox-terriers on wheels, and all the others. He was proud of these toys and of his part in their production. They were finer in every possible way – more ingeniously designed, constructed with greater craftsmanship, more fondly finished – than the torrent of shoddiness that had flooded them out of existence.

'I'll miss you too,' he said aloud in the overcrowded dining-room, staring down at the spaniel, Mandy, who was wagging her tail in the hope of receiving a rind of bacon. She would eat rinds only if they were so brittle that they broke between her teeth. This morning, Agnew knew, what he had left would not satisfy her: the bacon had not been overdone. He lit a cigarette, folded the *Irish Times*, which earlier he had been reading, and left the dining-room, pursued by the dog. 'I'm off now, Miss McShane,' he called out in the hall, and one of the sisters called back to him from the kitchen. Mandy, as she always did, followed him through the town to the toy factory, turning back when he reached the forecourt.

A woman called Mrs Whelan, who came to the factory three mornings a week to attend to whatever typing there was and to keep the books up to date, was to finish at the end of the week. She was there this morning, a prim, trim presence in navy-blue, conscientiously tapping out the last of the invoices. The final delivery was due to be dispatched that afternoon, for Cathal O'Neill had already laid down the peremptory instruction that further orders must not be accepted.

'Good morning, Mrs Whelan.'

'Good morning, sir.'

Interrupted for the briefest of moments, she went on typing. She would be extremely useful to someone else, Agnew reflected, if she managed to find a position that suited her. 'I think I'm going to start clearing out the inner office,' he said, passing into it reluctantly, for it was not a task he anticipated with any pleasure. What on earth was he going to do with himself? Fifty-one was far too young simply to retire, even if he could afford to. It was all very well saying he couldn't see himself in the fuel business, either coal or turf, but what alternative was there going to be? In the failing toy factory he had had a position, he had been of some small importance, and he had often wondered if he himself – and the predicament he must find himself in when the factory closed – hadn't been an element in his late employer's sentiment. Had Mr O'Neill lived, the toy factory might have struggled on until a convenient moment was reached, when its manager might gracefully retire. Still, a father's sentiment rarely passed to a son, nor could it be expected to.

He took his jacket off and hung it up. As he did so the telephone rang and the widow of his late and sentimental employer invited him to what she described as a very small party on Friday evening. It would be in his honour, he said to himself after he had politely accepted. It was the kind of thing people did; there might even be a presentation, in the conventional way, of cutlery or Waterford glass or a clock.

'Now, this is bloody ridiculous!' Cathal glared at his mother, squinting in his extreme rage.

She remembered that squint in his pram. She remembered how his face would turn scarlet before exploding like a volcano, how he would beat his fists against her when she tried to lift him up. His father had had a bad temper also, though over the years she had learnt to ignore it.

'It isn't ridiculous at all, Cathal.'

'You are fifty-nine years of age.'

'I'm only too well aware of that.'

'Agnew's our employee, for God's sake!' He said something else and then broke off, his shout becoming an incomprehensible stutter. He began again, calming down and collecting himself. 'My God, when I think of Agnew!'

'I invited Basil Agnew –'

'Basil? *Basil*?'

'You knew his name was Basil. B. J. Agnew. It's on all the letters.'

'In no way did I know the man's name was Basil. I didn't know what his bloody name was.'

'Don't be violent, Cathal.'

'Aw, for God's sake now!' He turned away from her. He crossed the Italianate drawing-room and stood with his back to her, morosely looking out of the window.

'I invited Basil Agnew to a little evening I had and he stayed on afterwards to help me clear up a bit. The Flanagans were there, and the Fitzfynnes and a few others. It was all quite above board, Cathal. Father Doherty was there, quite happy with the arrangement.'

'You were seen out at Rathfarran with Agnew. You were in Lynch's with him.'

'That was later on, the following Sunday week it was. And of course we were in Lynch's. We had two glasses of whiskey each in Lynch's, and then we had our supper there.'

'Will you for God's sake examine what you're doing? You hardly know Agnew.'

'I've known him for seventeen years.'

Cathal mentioned his father, who, God rest him, would be disgusted if he knew, and probably he did know. He could not understand, Cathal repeated for the third time in this tempestuous conversation, how any sane woman could behave like this.

'Well, I have behaved like this, Cathal. I have been asked a question by Basil Agnew and I have answered in the affirmative. I wanted to tell you before I spoke a word to Father Doherty.'

'Agnew's a Protestant.'

'We'll be married by Father Doherty. Basil isn't the least particular about matters like that.'

'I bet he isn't. The bloody man –'

'I must ask you, Cathal, not to keep referring to Basil Agnew as a bloody man. I do not refer to Thelma as a bloody woman. When you informed me in this very room that you intended to marry her I held my peace.'

'The man's after your money and that's all there's to it.'

'You're being unpleasant, Cathal.'

He almost spat. As a child, he had had a most disagreeable habit of spitting. His eyes savaged her as he continued violently to upbraid her and to insult the man she had agreed to marry. He left eventually, barging his way out of the drawing-room, shouting back at her from the hall before he barged his way out of the house.

That evening her two married daughters, Eileen in Dublin and Rose in Trim, telephoned her. They were more diplomatic than Cathal, as they had always been. They beseeched her not to be hasty; both offered to come and talk it over with her. She had written to them, she said; she was sorry Cathal had taken it upon himself to get in touch also, since she had particularly asked him not to. 'It's all in my letter,' she assured her daughters in turn. 'Everything about how I feel and how I've thought it carefully over.' The two men they'd married themselves were, after all, no great shakes. If you were honest you had to say that, one of them little better than a commercial traveller, the other reputed to be the worst veterinary surgeon in Trim. Yet she hadn't made much of a fuss when Eileen first brought her mousy little Liam to Arcangelo House, nor over Rose's Eddie, a younger version of Dessie Fitzfynne, with the same stories about Kerrymen and the same dull bonhomie. 'It'll work out grand,' she said to her daughters in turn. 'Was I ever a fool in anything I did?'

The following morning Thelma came round and in

her crude way said how flabbergasted she was. She sat there with her vacant expression and repeated three times that you could have knocked her down with a feather when Cathal had walked in the door and informed her that his mother was intending to marry Agnew. 'I couldn't close my mouth,' Thelma said. 'I was stirring custard in the kitchen and declare to God didn't the damn stuff burn on me. "She's after getting engaged to Agnew," he said, and if you'd given me a thousand pounds I couldn't go on with the stirring.'

Thelma's rigmarole continued, how Cathal had stormed about the kitchen, how he'd shouted at the children and knocked a pot of blackcurrant jam on to the floor with his elbow, how she'd had to sit down to recover herself. Then she lowered her voice as if there were other people in her mother-in-law's drawing-room. 'Isn't there a lot of talk, though, about what Agnew gets up to when he goes off to Dublin for the two days? Is it women he goes after?' While she spoke, Thelma nodded vehemently, answering her own question. She'd heard it for certain, she continued in the same subdued voice, that Agnew had women of a certain description up in Dublin.

'That's tittle-tattle, Thelma.'

'Ah sure, I'd say it was, all right. Still and all, Mrs O'Neill.'

'What Mr Agnew does with his own time is hardly the business of anyone except himself.'

'Ah sure, of course 'tisn't. It's only Cathal and myself was wondering.'

The moon that was Thelma's face, its saucer eyes

and jammy red mouth, the nose that resembled putty, was suddenly closer than Mrs O'Neill found agreeable. It was a way that Thelma had when she was endeavouring to be sincere.

'I had an uncle married late. Sure, the poor man ended demented.'

You are the stupidest creature God ever put breath into, Mrs O'Neill reflected, drawing herself back from her daughter-in-law's advancing features. She did not comment on Thelma's uncle any more than she had commented on the burning of the custard or the loss of the pot of blackcurrant jam.

'You know what I mean, Mrs O'Neill?' The subdued tones became a whisper. 'A horse-trainer's widow in Portarlington that went after the poor old devil's few pence.'

'Well, I'm most certainly not after Mr Agnew's few pence.'

'Ah no, I'm not saying that at all. I'd never say a thing like that, Mrs O'Neill, what you'd be after or what he'd be after. Sure, where'd I find the right to make statements the like of that?'

Thelma eventually went away. She would have been sent by Cathal, who would also have written to Siobhan. But Siobhan had always possessed a mind of her own and in due course a letter arrived from Philadelphia. *I'm delighted altogether at the news. I kind of hoped you'd do something like this.*

It had never, in the past, occurred to Agnew to get married. Nor would he have suggested it to his late employer's wife if he hadn't become aware that she wished him to. Marriage, she had clearly decided, would be the rescuing of both of them: she from her solitariness in Arcangelo House, he from the awkwardness of being unemployed. She had said she would like him to oversee the demolition of the toy factory and the creation of an apple orchard in its place. This enterprise was her own and had nothing to do with Cathal.

The women she played bridge with still addressed him friendlily when he met them on the street or in a shop. Her golfing companions – especially Flanagan and Fitzfynne – had even been enthusiastic. Butler-Regan had slapped him on the shoulders in the bar of the Commercial Hotel and said he was glad it hadn't been Corkin she'd gone for. Only Corkin had looked grumpy, not replying to Agnew's greeting when they met in Lawlor's one morning, both of them buying cigarettes. Dolores Fitzfynne telephoned him at the toy factory and said she was delighted. It was a good idea to plant an apple orchard on the site of the factory – Cox's and Beauty of Bath, Russets and Bramleys and Worcesters. In the fullness of time the orchard would become her own particular interest, as the toys had been her husband's and the turf-bogs were her son's. It was a pity the family were almost all opposed to the match, but naturally such a reaction was to be expected.

She was aware of eyes upon them when they danced together in the clubhouse bedecked with Christmas decorations. What did these people really think? Did all of them share, while appearing not to, the family's disapproval? Did fat Butler-Regan and fat Flanagan think she was ridiculous, at fifty-nine years of age, to be allowing a man to marry her for her money? Did Dolores Fitzfynne think so? Mrs Whelan, who had been his secretary for so long at the toy factory, always attended the Golf Club Annual Dance with her husband; the Misses McShane, his landladies for the same period of time in the terraced house called St Kevin's, came to help with the catering. Did these three women consider her beneath contempt because she'd trapped a slightly younger, attractive man as a companion for her advancing years?

'I've always liked the way you dance the quickstep,' she whispered.

'Always?'

'Yes, always.'

The confession felt disgraceful. Cathal and Thelma, dancing only yards away, would talk all night about it if they knew. With Corkin, she wouldn't have had to be unfaithful in that way.

'You're not entirely devoid of rhythm yourself.'

'I've always loved dancing, actually.'

Corkin would have asked for more, and for less. Some hint of man's pride would have caused him scrupulously to avoid touching a penny of her money, nor would he have wanted to go planting apple trees under her direction. But Corkin would have entered her bedroom and staked his claim there, and she could not have borne that.

'We'll be married this time next week,' he said. 'Do you realize that?'

'Unless you decide to take to the hills.'

'No, I'll not do that, Norah.'

The Artie Furlong Band, new to the clubhouse this year and already reckoned to be a success, played an old tune she loved, 'Smoke Gets in Your Eyes'. His step changed easily, he scarcely touched her as he guided her through the other dancers. Sweetman was appalling to dance with because of his perspiration troubles, Dessie Fitzfynne's knees were always driving themselves into you, Butler-Regan held you far too tight. She'd go on playing bridge and golf after they were married, no reason not to. He'd said he intended to continue exercising the Misses McShane's spaniel.

'You're sure about this?' he whispered, bending his long face closer to hers, smiling a little. 'You're absolutely sure, Norah?'

She remembered thinking how she couldn't imagine him ever calling her Norah, and how strange his own Christian name had felt when first she'd used it. She would never know him, she was aware of that; nor could he ever fully know her. There would never be the passion of love between them; all that must be done without.

'I'm sure all right.'

The music ceased. They went to get a drink and were joined immediately by the Fitzfynnes and Rita Flanagan. Thelma came up and said one of the children had spots all over his stomach. Cathal kept his distance.

'We're drinking to the happy couple,' Dessie Fitzfynne shouted, raising his glass. Thelma scuttled away, as if frightened to be seen anywhere near such a toast.

'Cheers to the both of you,' Rita Flanagan shrilled, and in another part of the decorated clubhouse Butler-Regan began to sing.

She smiled at the glasses that were raised towards them. 'That's very kind of you,' he said quietly. 'We're touched.'

She would have liked to add something, to have sorted out falsity from the truth. He was indeed marrying her for her money. But he, in return, was giving her a role that money could not purchase. Within a week the family would no longer possess her. Cathal's far-apart eyes would no longer dismiss her as a remnant of the dead.

'We're going to have an orchard, you know, where the toy factory is now.'

They looked a bit surprised, at first not quite grasping her meaning and then wondering why she should mention an orchard just then.

'Our wedding present to one another,' he explained. 'Norah's trees and I shall tend them.'

The band struck up again, drowning the raucous singing of Butler-Regan. Cathal at last approached his mother and asked her to dance, as every year he did on this Christmas occasion. But he did not at last say that he hoped it would work out all right, Agnew and herself in Arcangelo House. She had paid some price, Cathal believed, apart from the financial one. But Cathal, really, was not right and for him, too, she would have liked to sort out falsity from the truth.

*

'Well, that is that,' he said, turning off the television on a Sunday night, after he had returned from Dublin. He lurched a little as he moved towards her, holding out his packet of cigarettes. He had said, before their marriage, that he often became intoxicated in the course of these weekends. He met his friends and they went from place to place, all of them men who enjoyed the company of men. Sometimes, left alone, or unlucky in the new companions he had met, he wandered the quaysides of the city, thinking about the sailors on the ships. On the strand at Rathfarran his face had been averted when he told her this, and when he finished she had not spoken. Dessie Fitzfynne and Sweetman liked men's company also, she had thought, and so had her husband in his lifetime. But that, of course, was not the same.

'I don't think I'll go back there.' He swayed, like Flanagan did in drink. 'God knows, I don't want to.'

He always said that. He always offered her a cigarette after turning off the Sunday television. A moment later he made the renunciatory statement.

'It doesn't matter.' She tried to smile, imagining him in the public houses he had told her about, his dignified presence mocked by a man who was once particularly his friend, a waiter who no longer liked him.

'I dread for your sake that someone will find out one of these days. I hadn't thought of that when we married.'

'I knew what I was doing. You told me the truth, and you're honourable for that.'

When he'd told her she had not confessed a truth as

well: that clothes and make-up disguised a loss she found it hard to bear. She was haunted by herself, by the beauty that had been there in a hotel in Bray. Lingering in the clubhouse on these Sunday nights, she drank more gin and French than usual, knowing he would be tipsy, too, when he returned. Once they'd fallen asleep in their chairs, and she'd woken up at twenty past three and crept away to bed. He'd seemed like a child, one arm hanging down, fingers resting on the carpet. On the strand at Rathfarran he'd told her he never wanted to go to sleep on these Sunday nights because he hated waking up so. In his bedroom at St Kevin's, the door locked against indiscreet entrance by one or other of the Misses McShane, he had sat with the whiskey bottle he'd bought for the purpose in Dublin. She'd listened while he'd told her that; concerning herself, there'd been no need to say what she might have said because, being the man he was, he guessed.

They passed together through the hall of Arcangelo House and mounted the stairs to their separate bedrooms. They paused before they parted, offering in their tipsiness a vague, unstated reassurance. Tomorrow none of this would be mentioned; their common ground would not be traversed on a mundane Monday morning. For a moment on the landing outside their bedrooms they spoke of the orchard that would replace the toy factory, and the trees they would watch growing up.

Honeymoon in Tramore

They stayed in a boarding-house, St Agnes's, run by a Mrs Hurley. 'You have it written all over you!' this woman said when she opened the door to them. She eyed a speck of confetti on the lapel of his navy-blue suit and then glanced briefly at the rounding of Kitty's stomach. It was the summer of 1948, a warm afternoon in July.

Mrs Hurley was a middle-aged landlady in a brown coat, who apologized for the wellington boots she was wearing: she'd been brushing down the yard. Her fingernails were enamelled a vivid shade of pink, her hair was contained by a tidy blue hairnet which partially disguised an arrangement of pins and curling papers. They would be very happy in St Agnes's, she said; they'd have the place to themselves because there was no one else stopping in the house at the moment. When they were carrying their two suitcases upstairs she said that marriage was a God-given institution and added that her husband went to Mass every morning of his life, on his way to work with the county council. 'Your tea'll be on the table at six on the dot,' she said.

On their own, they embraced. He put his hand under his wife's skirt and felt for the warm flesh at the top of her stockings. 'Jesus, you're terrible,' she murmured thickly at him, as she had on the bus when he'd pressed himself close against her. She was sweating because of her condition and the July heat. Her face was sticky with perspiration, and small patches of it had developed on her dress, beneath each armpit. 'Jesus,' she whispered again. 'Oh Jesus, go easy now.'

He didn't want to go easy. They were free of the farm, and of her father and her aunt and her Uncle Ned Cauley. He had a right to his desires.

'That woman'll be listening,' she whispered in the same slurred voice, but it didn't matter if the woman was listening. It didn't even matter if the woman opened the door and walked in. The bed made creaking sounds when she wriggled away from him, saying again that he was terrible, giggling as she said it. The bedroom smelt of flies, as if the windows hadn't been opened for a long time. 'God, you're great, Kitty,' he said, his own voice thickening also.

He was thirty-three, Kitty two years older. At fifteen he had been taken from the orphans' home in Cork by Kitty's father and her Uncle Ned Cauley. The two men had let it be known that they could do with a young fellow on the farm, and Father Doran, who was their parish priest at that time, had made inquiries of Father Lyhane at the orphans' home on their behalf. 'Davy Toome's a good lad,' Father Lyhane had said, and a few weeks later, after the recommendation had been passed on to the farmers and after Father Doran had been assured that the candidate would be strong enough for farm-work, a label with that name on it had been attached to the boy and he'd been forwarded by train. 'And did you never do farm-work before?'

Kitty's Uncle Ned Cauley had asked, sitting beside him in the cart as they slowly progressed on the road from the railway junction. But Davy had never even seen fields with corn in them before, let alone taken part in farm-work. 'I'm thinking,' said Kitty's uncle, who'd spent an hour in Doolin's public house at the railway junction, 'that it could be we bought a pig in a poke.' He said it again in the kitchen when they arrived, while his wife and his brother-in-law were examining Davy, silently agreeing that he was not as strong as the priest had claimed. 'Will you for God's sake take off that label!' the woman said to him, and then, in a gentler voice, asked him about his name. She'd never heard of Toome before, she said, so he told them that his name had been given to him when the orphans' home had taken him in as an infant, that there'd been a priest connected with it then who'd had an interest in naming the orphans. His first name was in memory of St David. Toome meant a burial mound. 'Is he right in the head?' he afterwards heard Kitty's father asking his brother-in-law and her uncle replying that you wouldn't know, the way he was talking about burial mounds.

'Will you come on now, for heaven's sake!' Kitty rebuked him in the bedroom at St Agnes's. 'And let me take off my hat.'

She pushed him away from her and told him to open the window. It was she who had chosen Tramore for the weekend of their honeymoon, saying she'd heard it was lovely, with a sandy little beach. Kitty knew what she wanted, her aunt used to say, and you couldn't budge her when she made up her mind. 'Would you accompany me to Cork?' she had suggested one day four months ago. 'I'm a stranger to the city, Davy.' He hadn't been back to Cork since he'd come to the farm, and he didn't really know his way around it; but it turned out that Kitty had never been there at all. 'We'll fix it to go on a Saturday,' she said, and on the bus he felt proud to be sitting there with her, a big handsome girl, the daughter of his employer: he hoped that on the streets they'd maybe meet someone from the orphans' home. She'd looked out the window most of the time, not saying very much to him, her round face pink with excitement. She was good-looking in a way he admired, better-looking than any of the other girls at Mass, or the tinker girls whom he'd caught once stealing turnips from the field, who'd shouted over a hedge at him that their sister would marry him. Her hair was very fine and very black, like a dark mist encircling her face. He'd heard her aunt calling her sullen, but he'd never noticed that himself, even though sometimes a blankness came into her face and stayed there till she roused herself. Her three brothers had all been born with something wrong with them and had died in childhood, before he had come to the farm. Nobody mentioned them; he hadn't even known about her brothers until one of the men who came to help with the harvest referred to them in passing. Her mother had died giving birth to the last of them.

'Are you OK, pet?' Kitty said, putting lipstick on at the dressing-table. 'Isn't it great we're on our own?'

He leaned against the window-frame, looking at her,

seeing her in the looking-glass as well. She had to go to see a Mr Minogue, she'd said eventually on the bus, a chemist in McHenry Street.

'Great,' he said from the window.

'Can you hear the sea there?'

He shook his head. They'd found the chemist's shop, having had to ask for directions to McHenry Street. If her mother was alive she'd have accompanied her, she said all of a sudden, and then she said she couldn't go into the chemist's shop alone. Her voice became different. Her legs wouldn't have taken her, she said, and then she told him she was in trouble. Her aunt had found out about the chemist, she said, only she'd refused to accompany her. 'Take Toome to show you the way,' her aunt had said.

'Will we go down, pet?'

He moved to where she stood by the dressing-table but when he put his arms around her she said sharply that she didn't want to get messed up again. She'd spilt powder on the glass top of the dressing-table, the same peach shade that was on her cheeks. She'd put on perfume he could smell, a strong sweet smell that made him want to try again to put his arms around her. But already she had crossed the room to the door. She opened it and he followed her downstairs.

'I've done you black puddings,' Mrs Hurley said in the dining-room, placing before them plates of fried sausages and fried eggs and slices of the delicacy she spoke of.

'God, I love black pudding,' Kitty said, and he passed her his because as a boy in the orphans' home he had developed a revulsion for this dark composition of pig's blood and entrails. The table they sat at was empty of other guests, as Mrs Hurley had promised. He smiled at his bride across it. On the way downstairs she had kept repeating that this would be their first meal as husband and wife. She attached importance to the fact. She'd said it again as they sat down. Through the wooden hatch that opened into the kitchen the voice of Mrs Hurley could be heard raised in abuse, speaking about a greyhound.

'Are you hungry, pet?'

He wasn't; he shook his head.

'D'you know what it is,' Kitty said, cutting into a soda farl, 'I could eat the head off of a horse.'

A low mumble of protest had begun in the kitchen, which he guessed must emanate from Mrs Hurley's husband. 'Errah, have a pick of sense, will you?' the landlady stridently interrupted. 'Would any animal in its sane mind keep getting into a cement mixer?'

Kitty giggled. She'd nearly died, she said, when Mrs Kilfedder gave her a kiss at the wedding. 'One thing about Kilfedder,' she added, 'he keeps his hands to himself.'

At that moment a man in shirtsleeves entered the dining-room. He greeted them and introduced himself as Mr Hurley. He inquired if they'd like another pot of tea, already seizing the metal teapot and moving towards the hatch with it. They'd find St Agnes's restful, he said, no children for miles around. The hatch opened and Mrs Hurley's freshly rouged face appeared. She had removed her hairnet, and the hair it had controlled, now seen to be a shade of henna, fluffed elaborately about her head. 'Have they butter enough?' she demanded of her husband, in the same uncompromising tone she had employed when protesting about the activities of the greyhound. 'It's good country butter,' she shouted at her guests. 'Fresh as a daisy.'

'We have plenty,' Kitty replied. 'It's good butter all right, Mrs Hurley.'

The teapot was handed back through the hatch and placed on the table. 'There's a big attraction in Tramore tonight,' Mr Hurley said. 'Have you ever heard tell of the Carmodys?'

When they said they hadn't he told them that the Carmodys ran a Wall of Death that was reputed to be great entertainment. She had never seen a Wall of Death yet, Kitty said when he'd gone. 'D'you like the sausages, pet?'

He nodded, holding his cup out for tea. Under the table the calves of their legs were pressed together.

'Coddy Donnegan wanted to take me once, only I said I couldn't watch it.'

'Maybe we wouldn't bother in that case.'

'I'd watch anything with yourself, Davy. Maybe we'd walk down by the sea as well.'

He nodded again and she leaned forward to say she was feeling fine, a reference to the fact that she had recently been subject to bouts of sickness in her stomach. They'd have a few drinks after the Wall of Death and the walk, she suggested, in case it wouldn't look good, coming back to the bedroom too soon. She winked and nudged him with her knee. Under the table he put his hand on her lightly stockinged leg. 'Oh Jesus, lay off now,' she whispered.

It wasn't Coddy Donnegan, she'd told him in McHenry Street, standing outside the chemist's shop. She'd never been in love with Coddy Donnegan. She'd never been in love until the other thing happened, until there was a man taking her hand in a way Coddy Donnegan wouldn't do in a million years – a cousin of Father Tolan's, who was destined himself for the priesthood. He'd been about in the parish for the summer holidays; she'd have put down her life for him, she said. 'He'd marry me if he knew, Davy. He'd give up the priesthood, only I'd never tell him.'

They finished the meal Mrs Hurley had prepared for them. 'I'll just go upstairs a minute,' she said. 'I won't be a tick, pet.'

Waiting in the hall, Davy examined the pictures on the walls. A light burned beneath the Virgin and Child; there were reproductions of Victorian paintings, one of a match-seller, another of a shawled woman with a basket of lavender. He turned away from them, and the face of the chemist crept into his recollection: the jaw dark, the chin pimpled beneath a raw shave, eyes magnified behind heavily lensed spectacles, cheeks as pale as the white coat he wore. 'Come in,' Mr Minogue had welcomed them that day, knowing what they wanted although nothing had been said yet. It was the afternoon when his shop was closed, and he led them through the stillness of it into a room at the back, where there were no chairs to sit on, only a table with a rubber sheet on it. 'I take a grave risk,' Mr Minogue announced without preamble, his unsmiling countenance reflecting eloquently the gravity he spoke of. 'The assistance I offer you in your distress is offered for humanitarian reasons only. But the risk must be covered, you understand that? It is not of my own volition that I charge a fee.' While he spoke he did not remove his bulbously magnified eyes from their faces, revolving his stare in a circle around each, sliding it from one to the other. 'You may know the fee?' he said, and when Kitty placed the money before him his grey, closely barbered head bowed over the notes he counted. 'Yes, this is correct,' he said, speaking directly to Davy, clearly assuming him to be the father of the unwanted child and the source of the fee. He placed the notes in a wallet he'd taken out of the back pocket of his trousers, and jerked his head at Davy, indicating that he should return to the shop and wait there. But before Davy could do so both he and the abortionist were taken by surprise because without any warning whatsoever Kitty cried out that she couldn't do it. She would burn in hell for it, she shrieked in sudden, shrill, unexpected emotion; she could never confess it, there was no penance she could be given. 'I'd rather die as I stand, sir,' she said to Mr Minogue, and gave way to tears. They flooded on her flushed, round cheeks; the humane abortionist stood arrested, one hand still in the back pocket of his trousers. 'Hail Mary, Mother of God!' Kitty cried, shrill again. 'Sweet Mother, don't abandon me!' The money was handed back, no further word was spoken. Mr Minogue removed his white coat and led the way to the door of his shop, glancing before he opened it around the edge of an advertisement for liver salts pasted to its glass. The street was empty. As there had been no salutation, so there was no farewell.

'Are we right so?' Kitty said, descending the stairs.

He opened the hall door and they stepped out into the evening. It was warm and quiet on the terraced cul-de-sac, in which St Agnes's was the last house. They still couldn't hear the sea and Kitty said the waves wouldn't be big in that case. 'I'm sorry,' she'd said outside the chemist's shop, still sobbing, and then they'd walked for ages through the streets, before having a cup of tea in a café. She was calm by that time; it had never for a second occurred to her that she couldn't do it, she said, but the sin when she'd handed Mr Minogue the money had been like something alive in the room with them. 'I swear to God, Davy.' He'd said he understood, but in fact he didn't. He was confused because there was so much to take in – her being in trouble, the purpose of their journey being revealed, and then the episode with Mr Minogue. He was the man on the farm, the labourer who worked in the yard and the fields: it had been strange enough being asked to go to Cork with her. In the café, after she'd drunk two cups of tea, she said she was better. She ate a bun with currants in it, but he couldn't eat anything himself. Then he brought her to the orphans' home just to look at the outside of. 'God, Davy, what am I going to do?' she suddenly cried when they were standing there, as suddenly as she'd said in the back room of the chemist's that she couldn't go through with it.

'It's down at the strand,' a man told them when they asked about the Wall of Death. He pointed out the way, and soon they heard the music that accompanied it and the roar of the motor-cycle's engine. '*. . . to see again the moonlight over Clara*', moaned a tenor voice, robbed of its mellifluous quality by the scratching of a gramophone needle. '*. . . and to see the sun going down on Galway Bay*'. They paid the admission charge and climbed up rickety stairs, like a ladder, that led to the top of the circular wooden wall. A platform ran around the circumference, with a balustrade to prevent the jostling audience from falling into the pit below. 'God, it's great,' Kitty shouted above the noise, and Davy gave her arm a squeeze. A small, wizened man in red gaiters and black leather clothes, with a spotted red neckerchief, mounted the quivering motor-cycle that stood on its pedestal in the centre of the pit. He pushed it forward and ran it on to the incline at the bottom of the wall, gradually easing it on to the wall itself. Each circle he made increased the angle of his machine until in the end, close to the balustrade over which the audience leaned, he and his motor-cycle were horizontal. The timbers of the wall and of the platform shuddered, the roar of the engine was deafening. Waving above his head, the performer descended, the same circular motion in reverse. The audience clapped and threw coins into the pit. 'Are you OK?' Davy shouted, for in the excitement Kitty had closed her eyes. In the pit the motor-cycle was returned to its stand. The man bowed his gratitude for the money that still lay on the ground, and then threw out an arm in a sudden, dramatic gesture. He was joined immediately by a woman, dressed in red-and-black clothing also, who climbed on to the pillion of his motor-cycle and when it reached the centre of the wall clambered on to his back. She stood on his shoulders, with his spotted neckerchief streaming from between her teeth. Kitty screamed and closed her eyes again. More coins were thrown.

'Is she his wife, Davy?' Kitty asked as they walked away.

'I'd say she was.'

'Wouldn't it be shocking if she came off?'

'I'd say she wouldn't.'

'God, I love the smell of the sea, Davy.'

If she hadn't been wearing stockings she'd have paddled, she said, and he told her about a time they'd been taken from the orphans' home to the seaside at Courtmacsherry. He continued to tell her about this while they walked back to the town and went in search of a public house. They found one that was as quiet as St Agnes's, a murky place that Kitty said was cosy. Two elderly men sat at the counter, steadily drinking, not conversing. The publican was shifting sacks of meal in the grocery that adjoined the bar. Davy called out to him, ordering bottles of stout.

'Was it terrible in the orphans' home?' Kitty asked when he'd carried them to the table she was sitting at. 'Did you hate it the whole time?'

He said he hadn't. It hadn't been bad; he'd never known anywhere else until he came to the farm. 'Jeez, it looks like a prison,' she'd said that day, looking up at the orphans' home from the street.

'It's terrible, though, no family to turn to,' she said now. 'I have the half of it myself, with no mother.'

'You get used to the way it is.'

A week after their visit to Cork her aunt said to him in the yard that Kitty would marry him if he asked her. Her aunt stood there in the early-morning sunlight, a heavily made woman who was always dressed in black. She more than anyone, more than her husband or her brother or Kitty herself, knew that ever since he'd arrived at the farm with a label on him he'd had a notion of Kitty. The aunt was the sharpest of them, her eyes as black as her clothes, always watchful. She had noticed him looking at Kitty across the table when they all sat down to their dinner; he'd never been able to help looking at her, and it embarrassed him every time her aunt caught him. Did she guess that he lay in bed at night imagining Kitty's lips on his own, and the lovely white softness of her? They would have the farm between them was what she omitted to say in the yard because it was not necessary to say it: Kitty would inherit the farm since there was no one else, and if he married her he would no longer be the hired man, with the worst of the work always reserved for him. 'I'll ask her so,' he said, and because of the day there had been in Cork it was easier to pluck up the courage. Before that, Kitty had always ordered him about in the way her father and her uncle did when they all worked together at certain seasons, making hay or lifting the potatoes. He had never disliked her for it, any more than he'd ever felt he had a right to resent Coddy Donnegan's rusty old Vauxhall arriving in the yard and

Coddy Donnegan waiting in it, and the way he'd push open a door of the car when he heard the sound of her heels tip-tapping across the concrete. Father Tolan's cousin had never come near the farm; all that was a mystery.

'Would there be anything to eat in here, pet? Would they have biscuits?'

At the bar he ordered two more bottles of stout and inquired if biscuits could be supplied. The publican said he had ginger-snaps and went to the grocery to weigh out half a pound.

'Oh, great,' Kitty said. She crumbled one in her mouth. He poured out the stout. The day before her aunt had made her suggestion in the yard he had noticed Kitty going up to Coddy Donnegan after Mass, and Coddy Donnegan had turned away from her as if they'd had a quarrel, which was understandable in view of her friendship with Father Tolan's cousin. After that, Coddy Donnegan's Vauxhall never again drove up to the farm.

'We'll never forget our honeymoon,' Kitty said. 'I wish we had a camera. I'd love to take snaps of Tramore.'

He knew what she meant. For the rest of their lives they'd be at the farm, milking every morning and evening, taking the churns down to the creamery, ploughing and sowing and ditching. No matter how you fixed it there was never enough time, except for the couple of hours you took to go to Mass. He always rode to Mass on his bicycle, and on Sunday afternoons he rode over to Doolin's at the old railway junction, where no trains came any more. A new road passed by Doolin's now and on Sunday afternoons there would always be bicycles propped up against its window, and the same dozen or so faces inside. 'I hear you're marrying in,' one of the men said to him on the Sunday after Kitty agreed. 'More power to your elbow, Davy!' No one was displeased at his good fortune, in Doolin's or anywhere else. Father Tolan came up to the farm specially and walked down to the mangold field to shake his hand and to congratulate him. Even Ned Cauley, who rarely had a good word to say on any subject, wagged his head at him in an approving way.

'I love the taste of ginger-snaps and stout,' Kitty said. 'Did you know ginger-snaps were my favourite?'

'They're all the man had.'

Suddenly she asked him if he was happy. She repeated the question, putting it differently, asking him if he was contented in himself. He said he was.

'Will you ever forget the day we went to Cork, Davy?'

From her voice, he thought she was maybe getting drunk, that her condition made the stout go to her head. She was looking at him, giggling. She leaned closer to him and said that on the bus that day she'd thought to herself she wouldn't mind being married to him.

'You were good to me that day, Davy, d'you know that?'

'I always had a notion of you, Kitty.'

'I never noticed it till that day, pet. That was the first time I knew it.'

He went to the bar for two further bottles of stout. He had wondered if the men in Doolin's knew the state she was in, and if they imagined he was the man involved. The same applied where her father and her uncle were concerned, and Father Tolan. He didn't know if there'd been talk or not.

'Didn't it work out OK, in the end?' she said when he returned with the stout. She asked if there were any more biscuits and he went back to buy another quarter pound. When he returned to where they sat she said:

'Were you ever jealous of Coddy, pet?'

He nodded, pouring his stout from the bottle, and she laughed because she'd made him feel awkward. He looked away, wishing she hadn't brought up Coddy Donnegan. Then he turned and clumsily attempted to kiss her on the lips, but found them gritty with biscuit crumbs.

'Oh, Coddy's the right romantic! It was maybe ten or eleven times he said would we get married.'

He frowned, feeling that something wasn't quite right, yet for the moment uncertain as to what it was.

'Did I tell you poor Coddy cried?' she said. 'The day I told him I was marrying yourself?'

After that the conversation became confused. Kitty again mentioned her surprise when Mrs Kilfedder had embraced her at the wedding. She counted up the wedding guests, and said it must have been the biggest wedding for a long time. Her father had had to sell two bullocks to pay for it. 'Did you see the cut of old Feehy, without a collar or tie?' She went through all the guests then, commenting on their dress and wondering why other women hadn't embraced her. 'Will we take back a few bottles?' she suggested, nudging him and winking. 'Hey!' she called out to the publican. 'Put a dozen stout in a bag for us, Mister.'

When Davy had paid for them they left the public house, Kitty talking about a girl called Rose she'd been at the national school with, wondering where she was now. She hung on to his arm; he listened vaguely. Turning into the cul-de-sac, they met Mr Hurley exercising a greyhound, a dejected animal which in the course of conversation Mr Hurley said was worth a fortune. 'Is it the one that gets into the cement mixer?' Kitty asked, and Mr Hurley explained that the greyhound only got into the cement mixer the odd time.

Kitty laughed shrilly. The trouble with a habit like that, she pointed out, was that the creature might get turned into concrete. 'Will you take a stout, Mr Hurley? We brought home a few bottles.'

Mr Hurley instantly fell into step with them and when they arrived at the house he led them round to the back, incarcerating the greyhound in a shed on the way. 'Sit down on a chair,' he said in the kitchen and his wife produced glasses, saying it was unusual to have guests bringing drink back to St Agnes's, but where was the harm in it? 'Good luck!' said Mr Hurley.

Details of the Wall of Death were given, and details of the wedding. The unexpected embrace of Mrs Kilfedder was retailed, and reference made to Kitty's father singing 'Lily of Laguna' and to old Feehy without his collar or tie. 'Poor Coddy Donnegan hadn't the heart to attend,' Kitty said. 'He's a fellow from the slaughterhouse, Mrs Hurley. I went out with poor Coddy for three years.'

'They take it hard,' agreed Mrs Hurley.

'He cried, poor Coddy.'

'I had a similar case myself. A fellow by the name of O'Gorman.'

'A chancer,' said Mr Hurley beneath his breath. 'A real oiler.'

'O'Gorman could have charmed the leaves off the trees. I heard him called the handsomest man in Tramore.'

'The story is told,' Mr Hurley said in the same low voice, 'that he fecked a crucifix off a nun.'

'"Well, I'll never marry now," was what poor Coddy came out with when I told him. "I'll keep myself by for you, Kitty."'

'Where'd the point be in that, though?' Mrs Hurley interposed. 'Is poor Coddy a bit slow?'

'It's only his way of putting the thing, Mrs Hurley.'

The dozen bottles took an hour to drink, during which time Mr Hurley gave Davy a number of racing tips. He talked about famous greyhounds he had known or had even had a hand in the breeding of, but Davy was more interested in what the two women were discussing and was unable to prevent himself from listening. He heard Kitty saying the husband she'd married would do anything for you. He watched her leaning closer to Mrs Hurley and heard her referring to the cousin of Father Tolan. 'Errah, go on, are you serious?' Mrs Hurley exclaimed, glancing across at him, and he guessed at once what she'd been told – that the lapse of the priest's cousin had determined him in his vocation, that God had gained in the end.

'Held back all summer,' Mr Hurley continued. 'Put every penny in your pocket on him.'

Davy promised he would, although he had never in his life backed a horse and hadn't heard what the one Mr Hurley recommended was called. Kitty stood up and was swaying back and forth, her eyes blearily staring. 'I don't know should I have eaten the ginger-snaps,' she muttered uneasily, but Mrs Hurley said a ginger-snap never did anyone any harm. Mr Hurley was talking about another horse, and Davy kept nodding.

'You're a good man,' the landlady whispered as he went by her. He had one arm around Kitty, holding her up. He shook his head, silently disclaiming the goodness Mrs Hurley imbued him with.

'Are you all right?' he asked Kitty on the stairs, and she didn't reply until they were in the bedroom, when she said she wasn't. He lifted the china jug out of the basin on the wash-stand and after she had finished, being sick he carried the basin across the landing to the lavatory.

'God, I'm sorry, pet,' she managed to say before she fell asleep, lying across the bed.

Even though she couldn't hear him, he said it didn't matter. It had never occurred to him before that a cousin of Father Tolan's who came to the parish for his holidays must have attended Mass on Sundays, yet he had never seen him there. Nor had he ever heard anyone else but Kitty mention him. She had painted a picture of a saintly young man who had since become a priest, and in her befuddled state she'd wanted Mrs Hurley to know about him too. She had wanted Mrs Hurley to know that it wasn't anything crude that had occurred, like going with Coddy Donnegan in the back of a bloodstained Vauxhall.

'It's all right, Kitty.' He spoke aloud, sitting beside her on the bed, looking down into her face. In the bedroom there was the rancid smell of her vomit; her breath as he pulled the dress over her head was cloyed with it. Again he looked down into her face, under-standing why she had told the lies. When she'd approached Coddy Donnegan after Mass that day he'd probably retorted that she'd let herself get into that condition in order to catch him.

Davy stood up and slowly took his clothes off. He was lucky that she had gone with Coddy Donnegan because if she hadn't she wouldn't now be sleeping on their honeymoon bed. Once more he looked down into her face: for eighteen years she had seemed like a queen to him and now, miraculously, he had the right to kiss her. He straightened her slackened body, moving her arms and legs until she was lying comfortably. Slowly he pulled the bed-clothes up and turned the light out; then he lay beside her and caressed her in the darkness. He had come to the farm with a label round his neck; he had come out of nowhere, from rooms and corridors that were as bleakly anonymous as the orphan home's foundling inmates. He had been known as her father's hired man, but now he would be known as her husband. That was how people would refer to him, and in the end it wouldn't matter when she talked about Coddy Donnegan, or lowered her voice to mention the priest's cousin. It was natural that she should do so since she had gained less than he had from their marriage.

In Love with Ariadne

Images cluster, fragments make up the whole. The first of Barney's memories is an upturned butter-box – that particular shape, narrower at the bottom. It's in a corner of the garden where the grass grows high, where there are poppies, and pinks among the stones that edge a flowerbed. A dog pants, its paws stretched out on the grass, its tongue trailing from its mouth. Barney picks the pinks and decorates the dog with them, sticking them into its brindle fur. 'Oh, you are bold!' The hem of the skirt is blue, the shoes black. The hat Barney has thrown off is placed again on his head. He has a stick shaped like a finger, bent in the middle. It is hard and shiny and he likes it because of that. The sunshine is hot on his skin. There is a baby's perspiration.

Barney's mother died three years after his birth, but even so his childhood was not unhappy. In the garden at Lisscrea there was Charlie Redmond to talk to, and Nuala was in the kitchen. *Dr G. T. Prenderville* the brass plate on the wall by the hall door said, and all over the neighbourhood Barney's father was known for his patience and his kindness – a big man in a tweed suit, his greying hair brushed straight back, his forehead tanned, a watch-chain looped across his waistcoat. Charlie Redmond made up doggerel, and twice a day came to the kitchen for cups of tea, leaving behind him a basket of peas, or beetroot, or whatever was in season. Because of the slanderous nature of his doggerel, Nuala called him a holy terror.

Lisscrea House, standing by the roadside, was covered with virginia creeper. There were fields on one side and on the other the Mulpatricks' cottage. Beyond that was the Edderys' cottage, and an iron gate which separated it from Walsh's public house – single-storeyed and whitewashed like the cottages. Opposite, across the road, were the ruins of a square tower, with brambles growing through them. A mile to the west was the Catholic church, behind white railings, with a shrine glorifying the Virgin just inside the gates. All the rooms at Lisscrea were long and narrow, each with a different, flowered wallpaper. In the hall the patients sat on a row of chairs that stretched between the front door and the stairs, waiting silently until Dr Prenderville was ready. Sometimes a man would draw up a cart or a trap outside, or dismount from a bicycle, and the doorbell would jangle urgently. 'Always listen carefully to what's said at the door,' Dr Prenderville instructed Nuala. 'If I'm out, write a message down.'

When Barney was seven he went to school in Ballinadra, waiting every morning on the road for Kilroy's cart on its way to Ballinadra creamery with churns of milk. The bread van brought him back in the afternoon, and none of that changed until he was allowed to cycle – on Dr Prenderville's old B.S.A. with its saddle and handle-bars lowered. '*Up the airy mountain,*' Miss Bone's thin voice enunciated in the schoolroom.

Her features were pale, and slight; her fingers stained red with ink. *There goes Miss Bone*, Charlie Redmond's cruel doggerel recorded. *She's always alone.* Miss Bone was tender-hearted and said to be in love with Mr Gargan, the school's headmaster, a married man. *Quod erat demonstrandum*, Mr Gargan regularly repeated in gravelly tones.

On the Sunday before he made the journey to school on the B.S.A. for the first time Barney found his father listening to the wireless in the drawing-room, a thing he never did on a Sunday morning. Nuala was standing in the doorway with a dishcloth in her hand, listening also. They'd have to buy in tea, she said, because she'd heard it would be short, and Dr Prenderville said they'd have to keep the curtains drawn at night as a protection against being bombed from an aeroplane. Charlie Redmond had told Barney a few days before that the Germans were hard cases. The Germans were in league with the Italians, who ate stuff that looked like string. De Valera, Charlie Redmond said, would keep the country out of things.

The war that began then continued for the duration of Barney's time at school. Lisscrea was affected by the shortages that Nuala had anticipated; and de Valera did not surrender the will to remain at peace. It was during those years that Barney decided to follow in his father's and his grandfather's footsteps and become the doctor at Lisscrea.

'How're the digs?' Rouge Medlicott asked, and the Pole, Slovinski, again beckoned the waitress – not because he required more coffee but because he liked the look of her.

'Awful,' Barney said. 'I'm moving out.'

When he'd arrived in Dublin at the beginning of the term he found he had not been allocated a set of College rooms and had been obliged to settle for unsatisfactory lodgings in Dún Laoghaire. Greyhounds cluttered the stairs of this house, and broke into a general barking on imagined provocation. Two occupied a territory they had made their own beneath the dining-room table, their cold noses forever investigating whatever flesh they could find between the top of Barney's socks and the turn-ups of his trousers. Rouge Medlicott and Slovinski shared College rooms and at night pursued amorous adventures in O'Connell Street, picking up girls who'd been left in the lurch outside cinemas or ice-cream parlours.

'Why doesn't she come to me?' Slovinski demanded crossly, still waving at the waitress.

'Because you're bloody ugly,' Medlicott replied.

Students filled the café. They shouted to one another across plates of iced buns, their books on the floor beside their chairs, their gowns thrown anywhere. Long, trailing scarves in black and white indicated the extroverts of the Boat Club. Scholars were recognized by their earnest eyes, sizars by their poverty. Nigerians didn't mix. There were tablefuls of engineers and medical practitioners of the future, botanists and historians and linguists, geographers and eager divinity students. Rouge Medlicott and Slovinski were of an older generation, two of the many ex-servicemen of that time.

Among these were G.I.s and Canadians and Czechs, a couple of Scots, a solitary Egyptian, and balding Englishmen who talked about Cecil Sharp or played bridge.

'You meet me tonight,' Slovinski suggested in a peremptory manner having at last succeeded in summoning the waitress. 'What about tonight?'

'Tonight, sir?'

'We'll have oysters in Flynn's.'

'Oh God, you're shocking, sir!' cried the waitress, hurrying away.

Barney had got to know Slovinski and Rouge Medlicott through sitting next to them in biology lectures. He didn't think of them as friends exactly, but he enjoyed their company.

Medlicott had acquired his sobriquet because of the colour of his hair, a quiff of which trailed languorously over his forehead. There was a hint of flamboyance in his attire – usually a green velvet suit and waistcoat, a green shirt and a bulky green tie. His shoes were of soft, pale suede. He was English, and notably good-looking. Slovinski was small and bald, and still wore military uniform – a shade of blue – which Medlicott claimed he had bought in a Lost Property office. Slovinski could play part of Beethoven's Fifth Symphony on his teeth, with his thumbnails.

'I heard of digs,' Medlicott said. 'Out near the Zoo. That Dutch fellow was after them only he decided to go back to Holland instead.'

It was in this casual way that Barney first came to hear about Sinnott Street, and that evening he went out to inspect the lodgings. A woman with a carefully

powdered face and waved black hair opened the door
to him. A discreet smear of lipstick coloured her lips,
and there was a hint of eye-shadow beneath her
myopic-seeming eyes. She was wearing a flowered
overall, which she removed in the hall. Beneath was a
navy-blue skirt and a cream-coloured blouse that had
a fox-terrier brooch pinned to it. She folded the overall
and placed it on the hall-stand. Normally she would
not take in boarders, she explained, but the house was
too large, really, for herself and her mother and her
daughter, just the three of them. A pity to have rooms
and not use them, a pity to have them empty. The
trouble was that smaller houses were usually not in
districts she cared for. She led the way upstairs while
still speaking about the house and household. 'It's a
residence that's been in the Lenehan family for three
generations,' she said. 'That's another consideration.'

The door of a room on the second floor was opened.
'Fusty,' Mrs Lenehan said, and crossed to the window.
The bed was narrow, the bedstead of ornamental iron.
There was a wash-stand with an enamel basin on it
and a shaving mirror above it on the wall. There was a
wardrobe, a chest of drawers, two holy pictures, and a
chair. Patterned, worn linoleum partially covered the
floor, leaving a darkly varnished surround. There were
net curtains and a blind.

'The bathroom and W.C. are off the landing below,'
Mrs Lenehan said. In Mr Lenehan's childhood there
were two maids and a cook in this house, she went on,
and in her own day there'd always been a single maid
at least, and a scrubbing woman once a fortnight. Now

you couldn't get a servant for love nor money. She noticed Barney glancing at the fireplace, which contained an arrangement of red tissue paper. She said that in the old days there'd have been a fire laid in the grate every morning and coal blazing cheerfully every evening. Now, of course, that was out of the question. 'Thirty shillings would be fair, would it? Breakfast and six p.m. tea, the extra meal on a Sunday.'

Barney said he thought thirty shillings was a reasonable rent for what was offered.

'Of a Friday evening, Mr Prenderville. In advance would be fair, I think.'

'Yes, it would.'

'Best to have a clear arrangement, I always say. No chance for misunderstandings.'

Two days later Barney moved in. When he'd unpacked his suitcases and was waiting for the gong which Mrs Lenehan had told him would sound at six o'clock there was a knock on his door. 'I'm Ariadne,' Mrs Lenehan's daughter said, standing in the doorway with a bar of yellow soap in her hand. 'My mother said give you this.' She was dark-haired, about the same age as Barney. The rather long mauve dress she wore was trimmed with black, and snowy-white beads were looped several times around her neck. Her lips were painted, her hands and wrists delicately slender. Large brown eyes surveyed Barney frankly and with curiosity.

'Thanks very much,' he said, taking the bar of soap from her.

She nodded vaguely, seeming to be no longer interested in him. Quietly she closed the door, and he listened to her footfall on the stairs. As light as gossamer, he said to himself. He was aware of a pleasurable sensation, a tingling on the skin of his head. The girl had brought to the room a whiff of perfume, and it remained after she'd gone. Barney wanted to close the window to keep it with him, but he also wanted just to stand there.

The sounding of the gong roused him from this pleasant reverie. He had never much cared for the appearance of the girls – women sometimes – whom Medlicott and Slovinski admired in cafés or on the streets. Ariadne was different. There was an old-fashioned air about her, and an unusualness. As well, Barney considered her beautiful.

'Fennerty's the name,' a small, jaunty old woman said in the dining-room. Wiry white hair grew tidily on a flat-looking head; eyes like beads peered at Barney. 'Fennerty's the name,' she repeated. 'Mrs Lenehan's mother.'

Barney told her who he was. The last occupant of his room had been employed in Clery's bed-linen department, she replied, a youth called Con Malley from Carlow. Now that someone had replaced him, the house would again be full. There had been difficulty in regularly extracting the rent from Con Malley. 'Mrs Lenehan won't tolerate anything less than promptness,' the old woman warned.

A man of about fifty, wearing a navy-blue belted overcoat and tan gloves, entered the dining-room. 'How're you, Mr Sheehy?' Mrs Fennerty inquired.

Divesting himself of his coat and gloves and placing

them on the seat of a chair by the door, the man replied that he wasn't so good. He had a sharply receding chin, with features that had a receding look about them also, and closely clipped hair, nondescript as to colour. The removal of his coat revealed a brown pin-striped suit, with the corner of a handkerchief peeping from the top pocket, and a tiny badge, hardly noticeable, in the left lapel. This proclaimed Mr Sheehy's teetotalism, the emblem of the Pioneer movement.

'I had a bad debt,' Mr Sheehy said, sitting down at the table. Mrs Fennerty vacated a sagging armchair by the fire and took her place also. Ariadne entered with a laden tray, and placed plates of fried food in front of the three diners. Mrs Fennerty said the thick Yorkshire Relish had been finished the evening before, and when Ariadne returned to the dining-room a minute or so later with a metal teapot she brought a bottle of Yorkshire Relish as well. Neither she nor her mother joined the others at the dining-table.

'Did you know Mattie Higgins?' Mr Sheehy inquired of Mrs Fennerty. When he spoke he kept his teeth trapped behind his lips, as though nervous of their exposure. 'I sold him a wireless set. Three pounds fifteen. I had the price agreed with him, only when I brought it round all he had was a five-pound note. "I'll have that broken into tonight," he said. "Come back in the morning." Only didn't he die that night in his bed?'

Swiftly, the old woman crossed herself. 'You got caught with that one,' she said.

'I was round there at eight o'clock this morning, only

the place was in the hands of five big daughters. When I mentioned the wireless they ate the face off of me. A good Pye wireless gone west.'

Mrs Fennerty, still consuming her food, glanced across the room at the radio on the dumb-waiter in a corner. 'Is it a Pye Mrs Lenehan has?'

'It is.'

'I heard the Pye's the best.'

'I told that to the daughters. The one I sold him had only a few fag burns on the cabinet. The five of them laughed at me.'

'I know the type.'

'Five fat vultures, and your man still warming the bed.'

'Strumpets.'

The rest of the meal was taken in a silence that wasn't broken until Ariadne came to clear the table. 'I meant to have told you,' she remarked to Barney. 'Your window gets stuck at the top.'

He said it didn't matter. He had noticed her mother opening the bottom sash in preference to the top one, he added conversationally. It didn't matter in the least, he said.

'The top's stuck with paint,' Ariadne said.

Mrs Fennerty returned to her place by the fire. Mr Sheehy put on his navy-blue overcoat and his gloves and sat on the chair by the door. Skilfully, with the glass held at an angle, Mrs Fennerty poured out a bottle of stout that had been placed in the fender to warm. On her invitation, accompanied by a warning concerning hasty digestion, Barney occupied the second fireside armchair, feeling too shy to disobey. Mrs Fennerty lit a cigarette. She was a boarder the same as Mr Sheehy, she said. She paid her way, Mrs Lenehan's mother or not. That was why she sat down in the dining-room with Mr Sheehy and whoever the third boarder happened to be.

'Are you at Dowding's?' She referred to a commercial college that offered courses in accountancy and book-keeping, preparing its students for the bank and brewery examinations.

'No. Not Dowding's.' He explained that he was a medical student.

'A doctor buries his mistakes. Did you ever hear that one?' Mrs Fennerty laughed shrilly, and in a sociable way Barney laughed himself. Mr Sheehy remained impassive by the door. Barney wondered why he had taken up a position there, with his coat and gloves on.

'Six feet under, no questions asked,' Mrs Fennerty remarked, again laughing noisily.

Dressed to go out, Mrs Lenehan entered the dining-room, and Mr Sheehy's behaviour was explained. He rose to his feet, and when the pair had gone Mrs Fennerty said:

'Those two are doing a line. Up to the McKee Barracks every evening. Sheehy wouldn't part with the price of anything else. Turn round at the barracks, back by the Guards' Depot. Then he's down in the kitchen with her. That's Ned Sheehy for you.'

Barney nodded, not much interested in Mr Sheehy's courtship of Mrs Lenehan. Nevertheless the subject was pursued. 'Ned Sheehy has a post with the Hibernian

Insurance. That's how he'd be selling wireless sets to people. He calls in at houses a lot.'

'I see.'

'He's keen on houses all right. It's the house we're sitting in he has designs on, not Mrs Lenehan at all.'

'Oh, I'm sure –'

'If there's a man in Dublin that knows his bricks and mortar better than Ned Sheehy give me a gander at him.'

Barney said he didn't think he could supply the old woman with such a person, and she said that of course he couldn't. No flies on Ned Sheehy, she said, in spite of what you might think to look at him.

'She made a mistake the first time and she'll make another before she's finished. You could turn that one's head like the wind would turn a weather-cock.'

Ariadne came in with the *Evening Herald* and handed it to her grandmother. Barney smiled at her, but she didn't notice. Mrs Fennerty became engrossed in the newspaper. Barney went upstairs.

In time, he heard footsteps in the room above his, and knew they were Ariadne's. They crossed the room to the window. The blind was drawn down. Ariadne crossed the room again, back and forth, back and forth. He knew when she took her shoes off.

Handwritten notes clamoured for attention on the green baize of the board beside the porters' lodge: love letters, brief lines of rejection, relationships terminated, charges of treachery, a stranger's admiration confessed. The same envelope remained on the baize-covered board for months: *R. R. Woodley*, it said, but R. R. Woodley either did not exist or had long since ceased to be an undergraduate. *It is hard to find myself the way I am, and to be alone with not a soul to turn to*: a heart was laid bare within the dust-soiled envelope, its ache revealed to the general curiosity. But other notes, on torn half-sheets of exercise-paper, remained on the green board for only a few hours, disappearing for ever while they were still fresh.

Within their fire-warmed lodge the porters were a suspicious breed of men, well used to attempted circumvention of the law that began where their own rule did. They wore black velvet jockey caps; one carried a mace on ceremonial occasions. They saw to it that bicycles were wheeled through the vast archway they guarded, and that female undergraduates passed in and out during the permitted hours only, that their book was signed when this was necessary. In the archway itself, posters advertised dances and theatrical productions. Eminent visitors were announced. Societies' account sheets were published. There were reports of missionary work in Africa.

Beyond this entrance, dark façades loomed around a cobbled square. Loops of chain protected tidily shorn lawns. The Chapel stared stolidly at the pillars of the Examination Hall. Gold numerals lightened the blue face of the Dining Hall clock. A campanile rose fussily.

Barney attended the lectures of Bore McGusty and Professor Makepeace-Green and the elderly Dr Posse, who had been in the medical school in his father's time. Bore McGusty was a long-winded young man,

Professor Makepeace-Green a tetchily severe woman, who particularly objected to Slovinski reading the *Daily Sketch* during her lectures. The students of Barney's age keenly took notes and paid attention, but the recent shedding of years of discipline by the ex-servicemen left them careless of their academic obligations. 'Listen,' Slovinski regularly invited, interrupting Bore McGusty's dissertation on the functioning of the bile-ducts by playing Beethoven on his teeth.

The medical students favoured certain public houses: the International Bar, Ryan's in Duke Street, McFadden's. After an evening's drinking they danced in the Crystal Ballroom, or sat around pots of tea in the café attached to the Green cinema, where the private lives of their mentors were breezily speculated upon, and for the most part scorned. On such occasions Slovinski spoke of his wartime liaisons, and Medlicott retailed the appetites of a baker's widow, a Mrs Claudia Rigg of Bournemouth. For Barney – years later – this time in his life was as minutely preserved as his childhood at Lisscrea. And always, at the heart of the memory, was Mrs Lenehan's household in Sinnott Street.

'You've maybe not come across the name Ariadne before,' Mrs Lenehan said one morning in the hall, adding that she'd found it in a story in *Model Housekeeping*. Had a son been born instead of a daughter he'd have been christened Paul, that being a family name on her own side. As soon as she'd seen *Ariadne* written down she'd settled for it.

Barney liked the name also. He thought it suited

Mrs Lenehan's daughter, whom increasingly he found himself thinking about, particularly during the lectures of Bore McGusty and Professor Makepeace-Green. Ariadne, he soon discovered, didn't go out to work; her work was in her mother's house and it was there, during the lectures, that he imagined her. She assisted with the cleaning and the preparation of meals, and the washing-up afterwards. She was often on the stairs with a dust-pan and brush; she polished the brass on the front door. Every morning she set the dining-room fire, and lit it every evening. Once in a while she and her mother cleaned the windows.

Mrs Lenehan occasionally sang while she performed her household tasks. Ariadne didn't. There was no trace of reluctance in her expression, only a kind of vagueness: she had the look of a saint, Barney found himself thinking once, and the thought remained with him. In the dining-room he was usually the last to finish breakfast, deliberately dawdling. Ariadne came in with a tray and, seeing him still at the table, absorbed the time by damping the fire down with wet slack and picking up the mantelpiece ornaments and dusting them. Her elegant hands were as delicate as the porcelain she attended to, and her clothes never varied: the same shade of mauve combined repeatedly with mourner's black. 'Good evening, Mr Prenderville,' she sometimes whispered in the dusk of the hall, a fleeting figure passing from one closed door to another.

After he'd been in the lodgings a month Barney was familiar with every movement in the room above his. When Ariadne left it and did not return within a few minutes he said to himself that she was washing her hair, which he imagined wrapped in a towel, the way Nuala wrapped hers before she sat down to dry it at the range. He imagined the glow of an electric fire on Ariadne's long, damp tresses. Staring at a discoloured ceiling, he invaded her privacy, investing every sound she made with his speculations. Would she be sewing or embroidering, as Nuala did in the evening? Nuala pressed flowers between the pages of the medical encyclopaedia in the dining-room at Lisscrea, pansies and primulas she asked Charlie Redmond to bring from the garden. Barney wondered if Ariadne did that also. He guessed the moment when she lay down to sleep, and lay in the darkness himself, accompanying her to oblivion.

He didn't tell Rouge Medlicott and Slovinski, or anyone else, about Ariadne. In his letters to his father he mentioned Mrs Lenehan and Mrs Fennerty and Mr Sheehy: Ariadne mightn't have existed. Yet in the noisy cafés and the lecture-halls he continued to feel haunted by her, and wished she was there also. He left the house in Sinnott Street reluctantly each morning, and hurried back to it in the evenings.

'Ariadne.'

He addressed her on the first-floor landing one Sunday afternoon. His voice was little more than a whisper; they were shadows in the dim afternoon light. 'Ariadne,' he said again, delighting, while they were alone, in this repetition of her name.

'Yes, Mr Prenderville?'

Mrs Lenehan and Mr Sheehy spent Sunday afternoons with Mrs Fennerty in the dining-room, listening
to a radio commentary on a hurling or Gaelic football
match, the only time the dining-room wireless was
ever turned on. When it was over Mr Sheehy and
Mrs Lenehan went to the kitchen.

'Would you like to come for a walk, Ariadne?'

She did not reply at once. He gazed through the
gloom, hoping for the gleam of her smile. From the
dining-room came the faint sound of the commen-
tator's rapid, excited voice. Ariadne didn't smile. She
said:

'This minute, Mr Prenderville?'

'If you are doing nothing better.'

'I will put on my coat.'

He thought of her mother and Mr Sheehy as he
waited. He didn't know which direction the McKee
Barracks and the Civic Guards' Depot lay in, but wherever these places were he didn't want even to see them
in the distance. 'I'm ready,' Ariadne said, having de-
layed for no longer than a minute. Barney opened the
front door softly, and softly closed it behind them.
Damp autumn leaves lay thickly on the pavements,
blown into mounds and heaps. When the wind gusted,
more slipped from the branches above them and gently
descended. Ariadne's coat was another shade of mauve,
matching her headscarf. There'd been no need to leave
the house in that secret way, but they had done so
nonetheless, without exchanging a look.

'I love Sunday,' Ariadne said.

He said he liked the day also. He told her about

Sundays at Lisscrea because he didn't know how else
to interest her. His father and he would sit reading in
the drawing-room on a winter's afternoon, or in the
garden in the summer. Nuala would bring them tea,
and a cake made the day before. His father read books
that were sent to him by post from a lending library in
Dublin, novels by A. E. W. Mason and E. Phillips
Oppenheim and Sapper. Once, laying one down when
he had finished it, he changed his mind and handed it
to Barney. 'Try this,' he said, and after that they shared
the books that came by post. Barney was fourteen or
fifteen then.

'Your mother is not there, Mr Prenderville?'

'My mother died.'

He described Lisscrea to her: the long, narrow rooms
of the house, the garden where Charlie Redmond had
worked for as long as Barney could remember, the
patients in the hall. He mentioned the cottages next to
Lisscrea House, and Walsh's public house, and the
ruined tower he could see from his bedroom window.
He repeated a piece of Charlie Redmond's doggerel,
and described his prematurely wizened features and
Nuala's countrywoman's looks. He told Ariadne about
school at Ballinadra, the journey on the milk cart when
he was small, the return by the bread van in the afternoon, and then the inheriting of his father's old B.S.A.
bicycle. She'd never known a town like Ballinadra,
Ariadne said; she only knew Dublin.

'It isn't much,' he said, but she wanted to know, and
he tried to make a picture of the place for her: the
single street and the square, O'Kevin's hardware,

the grocers' shops that were bars as well, the statue of Father Mathew.

'A quiet place,' Ariadne said.

'Oh, a grave.'

She nodded solemnly. She could see the house, she said. She knew what he meant by virginia creeper. She could see his father clearly.

'What would you have done if I hadn't suggested a walk?'

'Stayed in my room.'

'Doing nothing, Ariadne?' He spoke lightly, almost teasing her. But she was still solemn and did not smile. Maybe tidying her drawers, she said. She called him Mr Prenderville again, and he asked her not to. 'My name's Barney.'

'Just Barney?'

'Barney Gregory.'

Again she nodded. They walked in silence. He said:

'Will you always help your mother in the house?'

'What else would I do?'

He didn't know. He wanted to suggest some work that was worthy of her, something better than carrying trays of food to the dining-room and sweeping the stair-carpet. Even work in a shop was more dignified than what she did, but he did not mention a shop. 'Perhaps a nurse.'

'I would be frightened to be a nurse. I'd be no good at it.'

'I'm sure you would, Ariadne.'

She would care tenderly. Her gentleness would be

a blessing. Her beauty would cheer the low spirits of the ill.

'Nuns are better at all that,' she said.

'Did you go to a convent, Ariadne?'

She nodded, and for a moment seemed lost in the memory the question inspired. When she spoke again her voice, for the first time, was eager. 'Will we walk to the convent, Barney? It isn't far away.'

'If you would like to.'

'We have to turn right when we come to Prussia Street.'

No one was about. The front doors of the houses they walked by were tightly closed against the world. Their footsteps were deadened by the sodden leaves.

'I like that colour you wear,' he said.

'An aunt left me her clothes.'

'An aunt?'

'A great-aunt, Aunt Loretta. Half of them she never wore. She loved that colour.'

'It suits you.'

'She used to say that.'

That was why her dresses, and the coat she wore now, were rather long for her. It was her clothes that gave her her old-fashioned air. Had she no clothes of her own? he wondered, but did not ask.

The convent was a cement building with silver-coloured railings in front of it. The blinds were drawn down in several of its windows; lace curtains ensured privacy in the others. A brass letter-box and knocker gleamed on a green side-door.

'Did you walk here every morning?' he asked.

'When I was small my father used to take me. It wasn't out of his way.'

She went on talking about that, and he formed a picture of her childhood, just as, a few moments ago, she had of his. He saw her, hand in hand with her father, hurrying through the early-morning streets. Her father had worked in Maguire's coal office in Easter Street. Sometimes they'd call in at a shop for his tobacco, half an ounce of Digger.

When they crossed the street he wanted to take her arm, but he didn't have the courage. They could walk to a bus stop, he suggested, and wait for a bus to O'Connell Street. They could have tea somewhere, one of the cinema cafés that were open on a Sunday. But she shook her head. She'd have to be getting back, she said.

They turned and walked the way they'd come, past the silent houses. A drizzle began. They didn't say much else.

'God, there's talent for you!' Medlicott exclaimed in the Crystal Ballroom, surveying the girls who stood against the walls. Slovinski conveyed a willowy woman of uncertain age on to the dance-floor, from which, a few minutes later, they disappeared and did not return. Some of the girls who were standing about glanced back at Medlicott, clearly considering him hand-some. He approached a lean-featured one with hair the colour of newly polished brass, not at all pretty, Barney considered.

Because he had no knowledge of dance-steps, the

partners Barney chose usually excused themselves after a minute or two. 'What line are you in?' a plump one, more tolerant than the others, inquired. He said he worked in a dry-cleaner's, Slovinski having warned him not to mention being a student in case the girls took fright. 'You can't dance,' the plump girl observed, and commenced to teach him.

When the end of the evening came she was still doing so. Medlicott had remained attached to the lean-featured girl, whom he confidently reported he had 'got going'. Outside the dance-hall Barney heard him complimenting her on her eyes, and felt embarrassed because he didn't want to have to tell the plump girl that she, too, had lovely eyes, which wouldn't have been true. Instead, he asked her her name. 'May,' she said.

Medlicott suggested that they should go out to Goatstown in a taxi, since the city bars were closed by now. There were fields in Goatstown, he reminded his companions: after they'd had a couple of nightcaps they could go for a walk through the fields in the moonlight. But May said her father would skin her if she got in late. She took Barney's arm. Her father was fierce-tempered, she confided.

The lean-faced girl didn't want to make the journey to Goatstown either, so Medlicott led her into an alleyway. They kissed one another in a doorway while May and Barney stood some distance away. When her father went wild, May said, nothing could hold him. 'All right,' Barney heard the lean-faced girl say.

A battered Ford car was parked at the far end of the

alleyway next to a skip full of builder's rubble. Medlicott and his companion approached it, she teetering on gold-coloured high heels. Medlicott opened one of the back doors. 'Come on in here, darling,' he invited.

It was difficult to know what to say to May, so Barney didn't say anything. She talked about her brothers and sisters; half listening, he imagined Ariadne at Lisscrea. He imagined being engaged to her, and introducing her to Nuala in the kitchen and Charlie Redmond in the garden. He saw himself walking along the road with her, and waiting while she attended Mass in the nearby church. He showed her Ballinadra – the rudimentary shops, the statue of Father Mathew in the square.

He glanced at the car and caught a glimpse of brassy hair through the back window. He would introduce her to the tender-hearted Miss Bone. He imagined Miss Bone dismounting from her bicycle outside O'Kevin's hardware. 'Welcome to Ballinadra, Ariadne,' she murmured in her gentle voice.

Three men had turned into the alleyway, and a moment later shouting began. A door of the car was wrenched open; clothing was seized and flung out. One of the lean girl's gold-coloured shoes bounced over the surface of the alleyway, coming to rest near the skip. 'Get that hooer out of my car,' a voice furiously commanded.

In spite of what was happening, Barney couldn't properly detach himself from his thoughts. He walked with Ariadne, from the town to Lisscrea House. On the way he showed her the Lackens' farm and the hay-shed where the Black and Tans had murdered a father and a son, and the ramshackle house at the end of a long avenue, where the bread van used to call every day when he got a lift in it back from school, where mad Mrs Boyce lived. Weeds flowered on the verges; it must have been summer.

'Get out of that bloody car!'

The garments that lay on the ground were pitched into the skip, with the shoe. Medlicott called out incomprehensibly, a humorous observation by the sound of it. 'D'you want your neck broken?' the same man shouted back at him. 'Get out of my property.'

'I'm off,' May said, and Barney walked with her to her bus stop, not properly listening while she told him that a girl who would enter a motor-car as easily as that would come to an unsavoury end. 'I'll look out for you in the Crystal,' she promised before they parted.

On the journey back to Sinnott Street Barney was accompanied by an impression, as from a fantasy, of May's plump body, breasts pressed against his chest, a knee touching one of his, the moist warmth of her palm. Such physical intimacy was not the kind he had ever associated with Ariadne, but as he approached his lodgings he knew he could not let the night pass without the greater reality of seeing her face, without – even for an instant – being again in her company.

When he arrived at Mrs Lenehan's house he continued to ascend the stairs after he'd reached the landing off which his room lay. Any moment a light might come on, he thought; any moment he would stand exposed and have to pretend he had made a mistake.

But the darkness continued, and he switched on no lights himself. Softly, he turned the handle of the door above his, and closed it, standing with his back to the panels. He could see nothing, but so close did the unspoken relationship feel that he half expected to hear his name whispered. That did not happen; he could not hear even the sound of breathing. He remained where he stood, prepared to do so for however many hours might pass before streaks of light showed on either side of the window blinds. He gazed at where he knew the bed must be, confirmed in this conjecture by the creeping twilight. He waited, with all the passion he possessed pressed into a longing to glimpse the features he had come to love. He would go at once then. One day, in some happy future, he would tell Ariadne of this night of adoration.

But as the room took form – the wardrobe, the bed, the wash-stand, the chest of drawers – he sensed, even before he could discern more than these outlines, that he was alone. No sleeping face rewarded his patience, no dark hair lay on the pillow. The window blinds were not drawn down. The bed was orderly, and covered. The room was tidy, as though abandoned.

Before the arrival of Professor Makepeace-Green the following morning, the episode in the alleyway and Slovinski's swift spiriting away of the willowy woman from the dance-hall floor were retailed. Barney was commiserated with because he had failed to take his chances. Rouge Medlicott and Slovinski, and several other ex-servicemen, gave him advice as to amorous advancement in the future. His preoccupied mood went unnoticed.

That evening, it was the old woman who told him. When he remarked upon Ariadne's absence in the dining-room she said their future needs in this respect would be attended to by a maid called Biddy whom Mrs Lenehan was in the process of employing. When he asked her where Ariadne had gone she said that Ariadne had always been religious.

'Religious?'

'Ariadne's working in the kitchen of the convent.'

Mr Sheehy came into the dining-room and removed his navy-blue overcoat and his tan gloves. A few minutes later Mrs Lenehan placed the plates of fried food in front of her lodgers, and then returned with the metal teapot. Mr Sheehy spoke of the houses he had visited during the day, in his capacity as agent for the Hibernian Insurance Company. Mrs Lenehan put her mother's bottle of stout to warm in the fender.

'Is Ariadne not going to live here any more?' Barney asked Mrs Fennerty when Mr Sheehy and Mrs Lenehan had gone out for their walk to the McKee Barracks.

'I'd say she'll stop in the convent now. Ariadne always liked that convent.'

'I know.'

Mrs Fennerty lit her evening cigarette. It was to be expected, she said. It was not a surprise.

'That she should go there?'

'After you took Ariadne out, Barney. You follow what I mean?'

He said he didn't. She nodded, fresh thoughts agreeing with what she had already stated. She poured her stout. She had never called him Barney before.

'It's called going out, Barney. Even if it's nothing very much.'

'Yes, but what's that to do with her working in the convent?'

'She didn't tell you about Lenehan? She didn't mention her father, Barney?'

'Yes, she did.'

'She didn't tell you he took his life?' The old woman crossed herself, her gesture as swift as it always was when she made it. She continued to pour her stout, expertly draining it down the side of the glass.

'No, she didn't tell me that.'

'When Ariadne was ten years old her father took his life in an upstairs room.'

'Why did he do that, Mrs Fennerty?'

'He was not a man I ever liked.' Again she paused, as though to dwell privately upon her aversion to her late son-in-law. 'Shame is the state Ariadne lives in.'

'Shame?'

'Can you remember when you were ten, Barney?'

He nodded. It was something they had in common, he'd said to Ariadne, that for both of them a parent had died. Any child had affection for a father, Mrs Fennerty was saying.

'Why did Mr Lenehan take his life?'

Mrs Fennerty did not reply. She sipped her stout. She stared into the glow of the fire, then threw her cigarette end into it. She said Mr Lenehan had feared arrest.

'Arrest?' he repeated, stupidly.

'There was an incident on a tram.' Again the old woman blessed herself. Her jauntiness had left her. She repeated what she'd told him the first evening he sat with her: that her daughter was a fool where men were concerned. 'At that time people looked at Ariadne on the street. When the girls at the convent shunned her the nuns were nice to her. She's never forgotten that.'

'What kind of an incident, Mrs Fennerty?'

'A child on a tram. They have expressions for that kind of thing. I don't even like to know them.'

He felt cold, even though he was close to the fire. It was as though he had been told, not of the death of Ariadne's father but of her own. He wished he had taken her arm when they went for their walk. He wished she'd said yes when he'd suggested they should have tea in a cinema café. Not so long ago he hadn't even known she existed, yet now he couldn't imagine not loving her.

'It would have been no good, Barney.'

He asked her what she meant, but she didn't answer. He knew anyway. It would have been no good because what seemed like a marvel of strangeness in Ariadne was damage wrought by shame. She had sensed his love, and fear had come, possibly revulsion. She would have hated it if he'd taken her arm, even if he'd danced with her, as he had with May.

'Ariadne'll stay there always now,' the old woman said, sipping more of her stout. Delicately, she wiped a smear of foam from her lips. It was a silver lining that there'd been the convent kitchen to go to, that the same nuns were there to be good to her.

'She'd still be here if I hadn't taken the room.'

'You were the first young man, Barney. You couldn't be held to blame.'

When Barney returned to Dublin from Lisscrea at the beginning of his second term he found, unexpectedly, that he had been allocated College rooms. He explained that in Sinnott Street, and Mrs Lenehan said it couldn't be helped. 'Mr Sheehy and myself are getting married,' she added in the hall.

Barney said he was glad, which was not untrue. Mr Sheehy had been drawn towards a woman's property; for her part, Mrs Lenehan needed more than a man could offer her on walks to the McKee Barracks. Mrs Lenehan had survived the past; she had not been damaged; second time round, she had settled for Mr Sheehy.

In the dining-room he said goodbye to Mrs Fennerty. There was a new young clerk in Ned Sheehy's office who was looking for digs, she said. He would take the vacant room, it wouldn't be empty for long. A student called Browder had moved into Ariadne's a week or so after her going. It hadn't been empty for long either.

It was snowing that evening. Huge flakes clung to Barney's overcoat as he walked to the convent, alone in the silence of the streets. Since Ariadne's going he had endlessly loitered by the convent, but its windows were always blank, as they were on that Sunday afternoon. Tonight, a dim light burned above the green side-door, but no curtain twitched as he scanned the grey façade, no footsteps disturbed the white expanse beyond the railings. In the depths of the ugly building were the strangeness and the beauty as he had known them, and for a moment he experienced what was left of his passion: a useless longing to change the circumstances there had been.

While he was still in Mrs Lenehan's house he had thought that somehow he might rescue Ariadne. It was a romantic urge, potent before love began to turn into regret. He had imagined himself ringing the convent bell, and again seeing Ariadne's face. He had imagined himself smiling at her with all the gentleness he possessed, and walking again with her; and persuading her, when time had passed, that love was possible. 'You'll get over her,' his father had said in the holidays, guessing only that there had been some girl.

A bus creeps through the snow: years later, for Barney, there is that image, a fragment in the cluster that makes the whole. It belongs with the upturned butter-box in the grass and the pinks in the brindle hair of the dog, with Rouge Medlicott and Slovinski, and the jockey-capped porters, and the blue-faced Dining Hall clock. A lone figure stares out into the blurred night, hating the good sense that draws him away from loitering gloomily outside a convent.

THE STORY OF PENGUIN CLASSICS

Before 1946 ... 'Classics' are mainly the domain of academics and students, without readable editions for everyone else. This all changes when a little-known classicist, E. V. Rieu, presents Penguin founder Allen Lane with the translation of Homer's Odyssey that he has been working on and reading to his wife Nelly in his spare time.

1946 The Odyssey becomes the first Penguin Classic published, and promptly sells three million copies. Suddenly, classic books are no longer for the privileged few.

1950s Rieu, now series editor, turns to professional writers for the best modern, readable translations, including Dorothy L. Sayers's *Inferno* and Robert Graves's *The Twelve Caesars*, which revives the salacious original.

1960s 1961 sees the arrival of the Penguin Modern Classics, showcasing the best twentieth-century writers from around the world. Rieu retires in 1964, hailing the Penguin Classics list as 'the greatest educative force of the 20th century'.

1970s A new generation of translators arrives to swell the Penguin Classics ranks, and the list grows to encompass more philosophy, religion, science, history and politics.

1980s The Penguin American Library joins the Classics stable, with titles such as *The Last of the Mohicans* safeguarded. Penguin Classics now offers the most comprehensive library of world literature available.

1990s Penguin Popular Classics are launched, offering readers budget editions of the greatest works of literature. Penguin Audiobooks brings the classics to a listening audience for the first time, and in 1999 the launch of the Penguin Classics website takes them online to an ever larger global readership.

The 21st Century Penguin Classics are rejacketed for the first time in nearly twenty years. This world famous series now consists of more than 1,300 titles, making the widest range of the best books ever written available to millions – and constantly redefining the meaning of what makes a 'classic'.

The Odyssey continues ...

The best books ever written

PENGUIN (P) CLASSICS

SINCE 1946

Find out more at www.penguinclassics.com